BOOK 4

MUST
LOVE
DIAMONDS

BY
STACEY JOY NETZEL

To Love and Protect

Must Love Diamonds Series, book 4

Copyright © 2020, Stacey Joy Netzel

Don't Dare a Diamond – excerpt

Copyright © 2020, Stacey Joy Netzel

Editor: Stacy D. Holmes

Cover Art: Cover Couture

ebook ISBN: 9781939143785

Print ISBN: 9781939143792

A brisk power-walk carried her to the stairwell door, her elevated breath visible in the winter air as she gripped the handle and leaned in with her shoulder while taking one final look to be sure no one had snuck up from behind.

The handle turned beneath her fingers and suddenly the door fell away from her shoulder. She stumbled inside, the top of her head colliding with something hard as a pair of arms grabbed her. A shriek tore from her throat as momentum sent her and her attacker careening backward into the wall on the opposite side.

Their jarring halt came with a masculine grunt that jump-started her fight and flight instincts. She kicked and twisted, pounding her fists against the body holding her captive.

"Jesus Christ," a rough voice cursed above her head.

She jerked her knee up into his groin and the man choked out a hoarse cry. He shoved her away and doubled over. The moment she regained her balance, she spun for the stairs as more curse words erupted from his mouth.

Shelby froze on the top step as the voice penetrated her haze of panic.

It had been years since she'd last heard it, but she recognized that voice.

After risking a glance over her shoulder, she turned to stare in disbelief. "Dev?"

He squinted up from his bent over position, his expression tight and furious until he recognized her. Well, even then, his expression didn't change much beyond a flicker of something dark in those stunning blue-green eyes of his. Probably disdain. Or contempt. Last time she'd seen Devante Torrez, he'd had plenty of both for her.

PRAISE FOR STACEY JOY NETZEL'S
OTHER WORK

"I laughed and cried, a great start to a new series, I can't wait for the next one." ~ FrostyJac, for **MUST LOVE FROSTING**

"I truly adored reading it! It's a feel-good, sexy & moving romance." ~ Doni, for **LOVE LOYAL AND TRUE**

"I had high hopes...and guess what? Hopes met with extra candy sprinkles on top just to make it that much better. With real insight to what makes an Oops Baby romance believable, **LOVE YOU, BABY** had me all in from the start." ~ Adria's Romance Reviews

"**KIDNAPPED**...starts off right away, and every page that follows is packed full of excitement that will keep you on the edge of your seat." ~ Danielle, The Book Whore Blog

"A thrill ride of an adventure and suspense, topped off with sizzling chemistry between the leads." ~ Helen, Amazon reviewer for **BETRAYED**

"Stacey Joy Netzel meets Indiana Jones. **CONNED** has it all - intrigue, suspense, danger and a incredible ending. Awesome writing, Awesome book." ~ Bev, Amazon Reviewer

OTHER TITLES BY STACEY JOY NETZEL

MUST LOVE DIAMONDS

Must Love Frosting

Love Loyal and True

Love You, Baby

To Love and Protect

Don't Dare a Diamond

ITALY INTRIGUE SERIES

Kidnapped*

Betrayed

Conned

*2012 Write Touch Readers' Award Winner as *Lost in Italy*

COLORADO TRUST SERIES

Evidence of Trust

Trust by Design

Trust in the Lawe

Shattered Trust

Dare to Trust

Vow of Trust

Illusion of Trust

WELCOME TO REDEMPTION SERIES

A Fair to Remember, Book 2

Grounds For Change, Book 4

The Heart of the Matter, Book 6

Hold On To Me, Book 8

Say You'll Marry Me, Book 10

(books 1,3,5,7,9 written by Donna Marie Rogers)

ROMANCING WISCONSIN SERIES

Mistletoe Mischief

Mistletoe Magic

Mistletoe Match-up

**Mistletoe Rules – short bonus story

Autumn Wish

Autumn Bliss

Autumn Kiss

**Autumn Glimmer – short bonus story

Spring Fling

Spring Serendipity

Spring Dreams

**Spring Spark – short bonus story

Summer Scandal

Summer Bride

Summer Secrets

**Summer Wager – short-ish bonus story

STAND ALONE ROMANCE TITLES

More Than a Kiss, contemporary romance

Chasin' Mason, contemporary western romance

Ditched Again, high school reunion novella

Dragonfly Dreams, Christmas novella

Nina, Beach Brides sweet contemporary novella

PARANORMAL ROMANCE TITLES

If Tombstones Could Talk, paranormal novella

Beneath Still Waters (Part One), paranormal novella

Rising Above (Still Waters Part Two), paranormal novella

FREE READ

Holding Out For a Hero

PUZZLE BOOK

Passion & Puzzles

a Word Search and Crossword Puzzle Book of Stacey Joy Netzel Romance books

DEDICATION

To Megan -
Your kindness will never be forgotten.

CHAPTER 1

nuckles white on the steering wheel, Shelby Diamond flicked her gaze to the rearview mirror as she turned into the hospital parking garage. The headlights behind her were gone, but instead of relief, a new rush of anxiety spiked her pulse.

Where had the car gone? Where would it be waiting for her next?

She circled the first couple floors, searching for a spot as close to the stairs as possible while checking the mirror every few seconds. When no other vehicles materialized, she forced her fingers open to get some blood flowing through them again. After one more time around, she found a space close enough on the fourth level.

She shot a nervous glance toward the elevator and stairwell. She didn't like having to descend two floors to reach the skywalk across to the hospital, but at least in the stairwell she could run if she had to.

You're being paranoid again. Everything is lit. It'll be fine.

These days, paranoia was becoming a constant, exhausting companion.

She surveyed her surroundings after she parked and shut off the engine. There was an older couple down the row getting into a vehicle, and a woman with a kid just getting into the elevator.

See? Nothing to worry about.

Still…she debated calling Asher to see if anyone was in the room with him and Honor and ask someone to come meet her. Just as quickly, she discarded the idea. They'd want to know why. Because, although it was already dark at six p.m. in January, it wasn't like she was visiting her brand new niece at one a.m. in the morning.

If she even gave a hint as to why she wanted an escort, the whole damn family would go into over-protective mode, and next thing she knew, Dad would have her moved back home under lock and key.

Well, maybe not quite that bad, but she'd had a hard enough time getting him and Mom to accept her moving to her own apartment last month, and she wasn't about to lose her hard-fought independence. It was the one instance being the baby of the family really sucked—and twice as bad with her dad being a U.S. Senator who had to deal with death threats because of his political work.

Because of that, she had compromised with her parents by letting them pick out an upscale, gated apartment complex halfway between their house and the veterinary hospital where she'd been working for the past three months. These days, she would admit to being grateful for the extra security when she went home at night—or sometimes at six-thirty in the morning if she worked a double shift. But only to herself.

Gathering her purse and keys, she checked the garage again before getting out of her car. She manually pressed the lock button and shut the door, and an additional press of the key fob sounded the reassuring beep to confirm the vehicle was secure. A brisk power-walk carried her toward the stairwell door, her elevated breath visible in the winter air as she continuously scanned the open expanse of concrete around her.

She gripped the handle and leaned in with her shoulder while taking one final look to be sure no one had snuck up from behind before she pushed through.

The handle turned beneath her fingers and suddenly the door fell away from her shoulder. She stumbled inside, the top of her head colliding with something hard at the same time a pair of arms grabbed her. A shriek tore from her throat as momentum sent her and her attacker careening backward into the wall on the opposite side.

Their jarring halt came with a masculine grunt that jump-started her fight and flight instincts. She kicked and twisted, pounding her fists against the body holding her captive.

"Jesus Christ," a rough voice cursed above her head.

She jerked her knee up into his groin and the man choked out a hoarse cry. He shoved her away and doubled over. The moment she regained her balance, she spun for the stairs as more curse words erupted from the man's mouth.

Shelby froze on the top step as the voice penetrated her haze of panic.

It had been years since she'd last heard it, but she recognized that voice.

After risking a glance over her shoulder, she turned to stare in disbelief. "Dev?"

He squinted up from his bent over position, his expression tight and furious until he recognized her. Well, even then, his expression didn't change much beyond a flicker of something dark in those stunning blue-green eyes of his. Probably disdain. Or contempt. Last time she'd seen Devante Torrez, he'd had plenty of both for her.

"What are you doing here?" The question came out all shocked and breathless seeing as her heart was still threatening to beat from her chest—though now it was for a completely different reason.

"Same as you, I imagine," he growled, bracing his palms on his knees.

He'd come to see her brother's baby? Before her?

"What the fuck was that all about?" He gave a short gesture toward the door.

"You scared me."

"Me? I opened the fucking door and you barreled into me. I was trying to keep us both from falling down the stairs."

"Well, I'm sorry," she retorted, the distain in his tone sparking her defenses. "How was I supposed to know?"

He started to straighten, only to halt with a pained grimace. It added lines around his eyes and pulled the corners of his mouth down. "You always freak out when someone opens a door?"

Nine years. She hadn't seen the man in nine years, and in less than a minute he'd reawakened all those feelings of shame and humiliation he'd left her with when he walked out of her bedroom when she was sixteen. But she was no

4

longer a shy, innocent little girl with hearts in her eyes—not entirely, at least. And she had nothing to be ashamed of right now.

Shelby raised her chin, his still bent position allowing her to glare down at him despite the solid eight inches he had over her five and a half feet.

"I thought someone was following me, and when you grabbed—" She broke off when he straightened to his full height, his gaze narrowing and sharpening.

"Who was following you?"

Without waiting for her to answer, he brushed past and yanked the door open. When he stepped through the doorway, her gaze was drawn down to the jerkiness of his movements, and she realized he was limping. Had she done that?

No. His brother, Reyes, had said he'd had surgery before being flown home from Landstuhl, Germany two days after Thanksgiving. She hadn't let herself think too much about how close he'd come to dying, but now she had the craziest notion of stepping forward to hug him and tell him she was sorry about what happened to him—even though she didn't know exactly *what* had happened.

"Shelby."

She jerked her gaze up to find his expression forged with a combination of anger and resentment. Heat flushed her body at having been caught staring at his legs.

"Who was following you?" he repeated through gritted teeth.

"No one. Forget it."

A muscle jerked in his clenched jaw. Clearly he didn't believe her, and who could blame him after her reaction to the entire situation.

She had to force herself not to fidget under his suspicious regard. Dev at twenty-one had been the epitome of the guy she'd wanted to lose her virginity to; she'd been in love with him for half her life. Dev at thirty was mature and war-hardened, and she found herself terrified and enthralled at the same time. He was still the most breathtakingly good-looking man she'd ever seen, but years in the Special Forces had sharpened his features and put ice chips in his eyes.

"Do you want me to walk you inside?"

It was an empty offer, made purely because his parents still worked for her parents, and he'd been raised to do the right thing. She knew, because he looked like he'd rather face a firing squad than spend another second in her presence.

The feeling is entirely mutual, buddy.

"I'll be fine." Then she grudgingly added, "I'm sorry if I hurt you before."

His lips stretched, though the result could hardly be called a smile. "I'll be fine."

Instead of exiting to the garage, he moved toward her, his steps slow and deliberate. She swallowed hard, fighting with everything she had to not look down at his limp. Feeling like he was testing her somehow, she stood her ground until he stopped right in front of her. It was damn near impossible to breathe with his gaze locked on hers, but she lifted her chin to show him—and herself—he didn't scare her.

"Excuse me."

She blinked at the raspy demand in his voice. "What?"

He gestured for her to move back as if she were an idiot. When she did, she nearly tripped on something at

6

her feet and looked down to see a cane with dark lettering burned into the wood.

"Oh. Sorry." She started to bend down to pick it up for him—

"*I. Got. It.*"

Flinching at the anger in his voice, she jerked upright and took another step back. He bent for the cane, the efforts of his movements evident in his tight expression and the fine sheen of sweat glistening on his forehead as he straightened.

Without another word, he pivoted and left her standing there, staring in shock...disbelief...mortification —until the door closed between them.

CHAPTER 2

*S*helby backed up a few steps and sagged against the wall. Scrubbing her hands over her face, she leaned her head back. *Holy shit.* Never in a million years would she have expected to see Dev *here*.

And, oh my, God, I kneed him in the balls!

The metallic clang of a door closing somewhere in the stairwell down below jerked her head upright. It was all the reminder she needed of where she was and why he'd scared her so badly in the first place.

Pushing off from the wall, she felt for her keys in her pocket and then pulled them out to fit them between her fingers as she skimmed down the steps. Her heart was thumping hard all over again by the time she reached the skywalk and rushed across to the busier hospital hallways. At the elevator bank, she stretched out her arm to punch the UP button when the doors slid open to reveal Merit, Mae, Ian, and Maverick.

"Hi, Shelby!" Seven-year-old Ian hopped off the elevator and gave her a hug right away.

"Hey." She turned a smile to her brother and sister-in-law over his head.

Merit frowned as he shifted the car carrier from his left hand to his right. "Everything okay, Bells?"

"Of course," she replied, though her pulse was still skipping like crazy. "Why?"

"Your face is all red."

From facing Dev and practically running through the hospital. "It is cold out, you know. Speaking of which, are you guys on your way out?"

"It's past dinnertime for two of my cranky boys and coming up fast for the third," Mae said.

Shelby laughed at the way her brother rolled his eyes. She leaned over to peek into the car seat carrier at her nephew, Maverick. He'd been born seven weeks early, but he'd grown like a weed these past two months. Now he was right where he should be if he'd been born on his due date.

The first time she'd seen her youngest brother holding his tiny little son, a pang of longing caught her by surprise, followed by a rush of pride for the man he'd become. And while she took care of animals smaller than her nephew at birth, it had taken her a month to work up the courage to hold the preemie infant.

"Ava is as big as Mav, and she was just born," Ian said. "Can you believe it?"

"And how big is that?"

He looked up at his mom.

"Seven pounds, eight ounces," Mae supplied. "But remember, Scoob, they were supposed to be born about the same time, so Mav is where he should be if he'd been born now, too."

Maverick let out a cry from his car seat carrier, and Merit grimaced. "We should go or we'll hear that the whole ride home."

"See you guys at brunch tomorrow?" Shelby asked.

"Yep," her brother confirmed as they headed for the skywalk.

She watched them go, wanting to ask if they'd seen Dev, but afraid to bring up his name when Merit had already noticed her flushed cheeks.

Thankfully, by the time she knocked on the door to Asher and Honor's room loud enough to be heard over the crying newborn, her pulse had settled back to normal.

"Hello? Aunt Shelby is here."

"Come on in," Honor called out. "Asher's on diaper duty."

Shelby entered and saw her older brother standing at a rolling bassinet, his back to the door as he dealt with the baby. She moved over to give her sister-in-law a hug. "Congratulations, Momma. How are you doing today?"

Honor had been in labor almost twelve hours yesterday before Ava had made her grand entrance into the world at six-fifty-seven p.m.

"Tired." And her smile showed it. "Though I did get to sleep some last night and again this afternoon."

"Well, I'm not going to stay long." Shelby walked over to peek at her new niece. She rubbed her hand on her brother's back as tears misted her eyes. "She's beautiful."

"Isn't she?" Asher gave her a proud papa grin as he swaddled her in a sunflower yellow, hand-knit blanket. She quickly quieted down when he cuddled her close to his chest, and he glanced up a minute later. "You want to hold her?"

"Definitely. I got all my practice in on Mav."

He turned to place his daughter in Shelby's arms. "Ava, meet your Auntie Bells."

"Hello, Ava," she whispered while gazing down at the tiny bundle. "So glad you finally decided to join us."

"Let's hope that isn't a sign of things to come with her," Honor said from the hospital bed. "I was getting desperate when we hit the second day past my due date."

"Tell me about it," Asher said as he went to lie next to his wife on the bed with a tired grunt. "She was begging me to have sex with her just to get the labor started."

Honor backhanded him on the chest. "I was not."

Shelby glanced up from the baby's sweet little face with a soft laugh. "Not that I want to know anything about your sex life, but I have heard that works."

"Told you," Asher said.

"I didn't doubt you." Her sister-in-law rolled her eyes as she met Shelby's gaze. "Now you know who was begging for sex. Like that was going to happen when I felt like a beached whale—looked like one, too."

Asher reached across to turn her face to him. "You were beautiful then, and you're beautiful now."

"That's sweet, Romeo, but it's gonna be a least six weeks."

"That's not why I said it," he defended.

She gave him a smile as she leaned in for a kiss. "I know."

Shelby peeked at them from under her lashes before returning her attention back to Ava's delicate little lashes fanned against her cheeks. That hint of envy tugged at her heart again. Someday she'd hold her own baby Diamond —or whatever her last name became.

That made her think of Dev again. There was a time she'd dreamed of becoming a *Torrez*. Until he broke her heart and walked away. He'd made sure to stay away, too. From her, anyway. She knew he'd kept in touch with her brothers over the years.

"Am I the last one to make it here?" she asked as Honor scooted down in the bed to lay her head on Asher's shoulder.

"Except for Grayson," he confirmed. "And while I don't expect we'll see him here at the hospital, what took you so long?"

"Some of us do work—and not for ourselves."

"On a Saturday?"

"It was the monthly feline spay and neuter day at the animal hospital to help keep the feral cat population in check. All hands on deck. "

"Ah. Got it. All the grandparents made it last night. Loyal and Roxanna, and Celia and Robert came this morning, and Merit and Mae left just before you got here."

"I ran into them downstairs."

"Don't forget Devante," Honor said with a yawn.

"Yeah, even Dev beat you to it, slacker."

Heat flared at the mere mention of his name, and she turned her face down to the baby. "I saw him on my way in, too. Kinda surprised, I might add." *Kinda—hah!*

"I ran into him downstairs on his way out of physical therapy and invited him up," her brother explained.

That made a lot more sense than him coming to the hospital just to see the baby. From what she'd heard, he'd been a bit of a recluse since coming home.

Since his medical discharge from the Army.

Not that she'd kept her ears peeled or anything when she'd heard her mother and his talking in the kitchen after Christmas.

Now, after seeing him, and seeing the after effects of what he'd gone through, she wondered if she should've gone to see him.

One split-second flash of his cold, angry eyes made her shiver as if a winter wind had snaked down her spine. No. He wouldn't have welcomed her visit.

A soft snore drew her gaze from the baby's face. While it was her brother who'd made the sound, another yawn from Honor told her it was time to let them have some peace and quiet. Ava had fallen asleep in her arms, and remained sleeping when she laid her in the bassinet. Shelby gently rolled it next to the bed, silently waved goodbye to her sister-in-law's whispered, "Thank you," and left.

She'd send Asher a text later and plan a longer visit when they were home and settled in.

Her pulse kicked up a notch as she made her way back to her vehicle in the parking garage. At first, it was because she couldn't help recalling the encounter with Dev. Once she exited the stairwell, anxiety returned with each hurried step across the cold concrete structure. Her hand shook as she got in the car, slammed the door, and clicked the locks.

She backed out and started for the exit when she noticed a piece of paper fluttering under her windshield wiper. Her stomach lurched as she braked and reached for the door handle, only to freeze. Stopping here and getting out would only make her vulnerable.

Shelby stepped on the gas again, darting her gaze all

around while leaving the parking garage. Her mind churned as she eyed the paper in between checking the rearview mirror to make sure no one followed her home.

Who had put it there? Why? What was on it?

The edge flapped back and forth, taunting her the entire drive until she passed through the security gates of her apartment complex. She parked in her garage bay, grabbed her things, and stepped out of the car. Her hand shook as she snatched the paper from under the wiper, but she didn't read it until she was in the safety of her home, with the doors deadbolted and all the lights on.

Opening up the sheet, she read the words as terror twisted her stomach into a knot.

One choice made the opposite way can be the difference between life and death.

CHAPTER 3

$\mathcal{D}$evante glanced at the flash of his cell phone screen while filling his travel mug. As he put the pot back on the burner and switched off the machine, he clicked on the text from his brother. Probably just letting him know he would be there to pick him up for their winter camping trip in a few minutes.

Reyes: *Hey, can you pick me up instead? My Jeep doesn't sound right.*

"Fuck," he muttered.

Reyes lived in the apartment above the stables at the Diamond estate. And today was Sunday, which meant most, if not all, of the Diamonds would be gathering at the main house for their weekly family brunch. Knowing the senator and Janine were home because of Asher and Honor having their second grandchild, it was pretty much guaranteed to be *all*.

He typed out a quick reply to his brother: *Maybe we should just skip it.*

After a long minute, Reyes replied: *Why can't you pick me up?*

Because he was a fucking wuss. Because since running into Shelby at the hospital last night, he hadn't been able to get her out of his fucking mind. Only it wasn't the bundled-up image of her from the stairwell that kept him awake half the night. Nope. It was the vision of Shelby at sixteen that had haunted his dreams off and on for the past nine years.

Beautiful. Innocent. Kneeling on her pink princess bed in a nude satin slip with black lace on the neck and hem. With her sleek, dark hair falling down her back, there had been nothing to hide the way her full breasts stretched the material over dark, pebbled nipples. The shadowy triangle at the juncture of her pale thighs had also been visible through the thin material.

His hungry gaze had eaten up the sexy sight while his twenty-one year old self summoned every fucking ounce of discipline he'd acquired in basic training, advanced individual training, and the Special Forces Qualification Course he'd recently completed.

S.E.R.E tactics were especially helpful. Survival, Evasion, Resistance and Escape.

She'd offered herself to him with those sensual brown eyes of hers swimming in hope and nervousness. And he'd been a complete bastard by yelling at her before storming out of the Diamond mansion. He'd done it for her own good—and his—and hadn't returned since.

But he'd sure as hell looked back.

Almost every damn day.

Sometimes twice.

He had worried he'd run into her when Asher insisted

he go up to the fifth floor to see the baby and meet his wife. Once he'd crossed the skywalk and started up the parking garage stairs, he'd figured he was in the clear and put her out of his mind. Not so hard when he'd been in pain because two flights of stairs after physical therapy had been a stupid macho mistake.

Seeing Shelby in the stairwell had been a shock, and not only because she'd nearly castrated him with her knee. And damn it, she was still beautiful enough to take his breath away. He couldn't help thinking, at twenty-five, she was now a woman. Of legal age and consent.

Except, he still couldn't act on the desire that had flared to life the instant he saw her again. For one, his parents still worked for her parents. Second, she wasn't the type he could mess around with and then move on. Shelby deserved better, and his career didn't allow for more than fun and done.

What career? The army doesn't want you anymore, remember?

He frowned at the brutal reminder.

Guess that opened up his relationship possibilities—except for the fact he had nothing to offer her.

Anyone. I've got nothing to offer anyone.

His fingers curled into a fist. Because when he didn't dream about Shelby, what kept him awake at night was a whole hell of a lot of shit he wouldn't dump on anyone other than his therapist. And only him because he got paid to listen.

At sixteen, Shelby had looked at him with a heat in her golden-brown eyes that belied her innocence. Two nights ago, she'd raised that beautiful gaze from his damaged leg to reveal nothing but pity. That look rubbed him raw like

17

wet sand stuck in his boxer briefs with ten miles to go to the rendezvous point after a mission.

The ring of his cell phone jerked him back to the present. Seeing his brother's name, he winced as he answered the call. "Yeah."

"What's up?" Reyes demanded. "You coming or not?"

His tone had an edge of desperation Dev recognized. He'd gone through some shit on deployment a few years ago and was still figuring things out. Great. How the fuck was he supposed to say no when he knew his baby brother needed this trip as much as he probably did?

"Yeah," he agreed with a soft sigh. "I'll be over shortly."

"Good." Reyes' usual smile returned to his voice. "Mom baked chocolate chunk cookies this morning. She said we should stop up at the main house to grab some on our way out."

"Forget the cookies," Dev stated even as his mouth watered at the thought. No way was he going near the main house today. "We don't need 'em."

"Speak for yourself."

He clenched his jaw. "Fine. Then go get them before I get there."

"Whoa. Okay. What's the big deal?"

He drew in a breath to rein in his frustration. "Nothing. Just be ready to go when I get there." Without waiting for a reply, he hung up and grabbed his stuff by the door to load into his truck.

On the drive over, the roads were slick from a couple inches of snow the night before, though the mid-morning sun had started the melting process in areas not shaded by trees.

Dev made the turn that would take him to the

Diamond estate, his pulse picking up a bit as he got closer. All he had to do was drive to the stables to get Rey and drive back out again. If he did see Shelby, at most it would be a glimpse from a distance. No big deal. They were probably eating brunch already anyway.

He blew out a breath and eased his grip on the wheel as he headed around the final turn before their driveway. As soon as he rounded the curve, the sight of a small, white SUV sticking up at an angle from the low ditch on the opposite side of the road made him brake. Flipping on his hazards, he checked to make sure the road was clear before pulling over by the vehicle.

There were no footprints outside the SUV, and the driver was still inside and appeared to be moving around, so he guessed the accident had just happened. Noting the steep angle of the ditch, he grabbed his cane while opening the door so he could go check if everyone was okay.

He was almost to the vehicle when the sight of familiar long, dark, Diamond hair made his pulse skip. He cursed under his breath as Shelby turned her head and her frightened gaze met his through the window.

Relief flashed across her features, then her expression shuttered as she ducked her head while opening the door.

"Are you okay?" he asked.

"I'm fine." Frustration rang in her voice. "I was just about to call up to the house."

When she got out of the SUV, Dev raked his gaze down the length of her body. He noted a pair of boots that were definitely not made for winter, then skimmed back up again to complete his swift assessment that was second nature after twelve years in the military, nine in the Special Forces.

No visible sign of blood or other injuries. She appeared rattled, but also fully alert.

He leaned a little closer to get a better look at her eyes, but she pulled back.

"Did you hit your head or anything?"

"No. Just kinda slid down in here."

He recalled the flash of fear when he'd first shown up. Had he misread that, or was she afraid of him?

That possibility brought a frown as he glanced back at the road. It deepened when he saw the whole section of road was bathed in sunlight, and the plowed asphalt was completely clear of any snow. "What happened?"

"I don't really know. The steering wheel suddenly locked up on me, and I couldn't make the curve."

Dev turned back at the mixture of anxiety and confusion in her voice. "What do you mean it locked up?"

She gestured sharply toward the SUV like he'd asked a dumb question. "It locked up. I couldn't turn the wheel and didn't hit the brakes soon enough and ended up here. I know it's stupid, but—"

Her defensive tone of voice triggered his. "I didn't say it was stupid."

"It's what you were thinking."

His fingers tightened on the handle of his cane as she glared at him. "You have no idea what I was thinking."

"Fine." She twisted away. "It's what *I* was thinking. I've driven enough on bad roads to know not to panic."

"You said it was the steering," he reminded.

"It was. That's why it freaked me out and threw me off."

"Literally," he muttered under his breath.

"I'm not a bad driver," she insisted.

"I didn't say that either. Stop putting words in my mouth." Dev stepped back to bend and look under the vehicle, then checked out the back to see a hitch on the bumper. "I have a chain in the back of my truck if you want me to pull you out."

She'd moved up beside him, but as she shifted her weight, her fancy boot slid on the incline of the ditch. He quickly reached out to steady her. Their gazes collided for a breath-stealing moment before she dipped her chin and pulled free.

"I can call the guys up at the house."

Much as he wished he could leave it to her dad and brothers, his conscience wouldn't let him drive away even with them only two minutes away.

Then he realized she was staring at his cane, and fury ignited that she thought he wasn't capable. "I can pull your fucking car out of the ditch, Shelby."

Her head jerked up, gaze narrowed. "You don't have to swear at me, Dev."

"Then quit looking at me like I'm crippled."

Her eyes went wide. "I'm not."

He leaned on his cane while raising his eyebrows. Her jaw flexed as she kept her gaze locked with his. But he could tell she wanted to look down again.

"Fine." She crossed her arms and leaned against the back of her vehicle. "Have at it."

After texting his brother he'd be few minutes late, he went to pull the thick chain from the back of his truck. With Shelby watching, he was hyper-conscious of every

21

glitch in his step, especially since he had to set his cane aside to attach the chain to the hitch on his truck.

Metallic clinks brought him around to see she'd stepped forward to grab the other end to drag to her vehicle. When he realized he'd paused to check out the fit of her jeans as she bent over by the hitch, he shook his head before joining her to make sure the chain was secure.

"Go ahead and get in your vehicle," he instructed once he was sure it would hold. "Just put it in neutral and keep the wheels straight. I should be able to pull you right out."

A few minutes later, he had her vehicle back on the road, and got out of his truck to disconnect the chain once more. Shelby unhooked it from her hitch and met him halfway to hand it over. Being a member of a close-knit team for nine years where everyone pulled their weight had him grudgingly impressed with her willingness to help and not simply leave it to him. He'd seen the way she grew up—the Diamond kids hadn't been spoiled brats, but they certainly hadn't wanted for anything, either.

"Maybe you could drive my car?" she suggested. "It seems to be running okay, but the steering is still nearly impossible."

"You're good to drive my truck?"

"Yep."

"All right. I'll meet you there. I was on my way to pick up Reyes, anyway."

"Thank you."

He gave a curt nod, and they switched vehicles. At the last minute, curiosity had Dev popping her hood. He checked a few things before slamming the hood once more. Shelby was getting out of his truck again, and he motioned her back inside.

"I'll meet you there," he repeated sharply.

She frowned, but got back in and followed him the rest of the way to her parents' house. The steering took considerable effort even from him, and he could see where if she wasn't expecting it, she wouldn't have been able to make that turn. He called Reyes to meet him at the garage of the main house and see if there was an empty stall.

All the family cars were parked in the huge horseshoe drive in front of the main entrance, but Dev drove around to the back. His brother waited outside one of the open garage doors, and he pulled Shelby's SUV into the empty space.

Reyes met him at the driver's side when he got out, and he asked him to confirm what he thought he'd seen under the hood. A moment later, his brother's solemn gaze rose to his, and he nodded as Shelby joined them.

"I appreciate the help, Dev, but you guys don't have to bother with my car. I'll call our mechanic to come deal with it."

Dev pushed up from the engine and faced her. "Who has access to your vehicle?"

Her brow dipped down as her gaze shifted to the engine, Reyes, and then back to him. "What? Why?"

"Your power steering fluid line looks like it's been tampered with."

Her eyes widened, and her face paled. "Tampered with?"

"Cut."

"Seriously?"

23

Reyes nodded when she glanced at him, and then she frowned at the engine again. "I, um...I have an indoor garage bay at my apartment, and the building is gated with good security. My dad made sure of that."

"You live alone?" Dev asked. "No roommate?"

She shook her head as she crossed her arms over her stomach. The way she hunched her shoulders it appeared she was trying to hide and his gut tightened. He'd bet money she was lying about something.

CHAPTER 4

Shelby swallowed hard as nausea welled up inside. She'd hoped the little incidences she'd been dealing with over the past few months were nothing, or not connected, and it would all just go away. Instead, the situation was only getting worse.

"What about at work?" Reyes asked. "Do you have any issues with co-workers?"

She shook her head numbly. Was she really having this conversation? "No. And the animal hospital has a regular parking lot, but it's pretty open. I can't imagine someone doing something where anyone might see them."

"You'd be surprised what people will do," Dev said roughly.

His cold tone sent a shiver down her spine. She knew he'd seen his share of evils people were capable of, but she didn't get why he seemed angry at her. Like before, when she'd said she'd call her brothers to help, and he'd accused her of treating him like a cripple. She hadn't wanted to

25

impose on him when her family was only a half-mile away, but he hadn't given her much of a chance to explain.

"Who was following you last night?"

She jerked her gaze to Dev's, surprised he'd remembered that.

Reyes leaned against the bumper with a frown. "Someone was following you?"

Hugging her arms tighter over her stomach, she shrugged uncomfortably. "I think so, though I had hoped it was just that I've been feeling a little paranoid lately."

"Why?" Dev demanded.

"It's stupid really."

"What happened, Shelby?"

Clearly, he wasn't going to let up on the interrogation until he got an answer. And yes, his intensity definitely made it feel like an interrogation.

"I got flowers a couple times without a card. At work, and once at home. And there were some hang up calls from numbers I don't know, but I figured they were telemarketers."

"That's it?" Reyes asked at the same time Dev demanded, "What else?"

Of course, he'd know there was more. "A few times I've felt like someone is watching me. Only when I'm out though, because I keep everything closed up at home. Doors dead-bolted, shades drawn." To the point home was beginning to feel like a cave. Or a prison.

"And?" Dev arched his eyebrows.

She flicked her gaze to his and away again, afraid he'd see too much. "What makes you think there's more than that?"

"Because you've always been level-headed and avoided drama. If this is bothering you, there's more."

Damn, he was good. With a heavy sigh, she reached into her jeans pocket and pulled out the note that had been under her wiper blade. His jaw tightened as he read it with Reyes looking over his shoulder.

The words rolled through her head, having been burned into her brain after reading them dozens of times last night.

One choice made the opposite way can be the difference between life and death.

Dev's stormy blue-green gaze rose to hers. "When did you get this?"

"It was on my car at the hospital."

"Last night?"

When she nodded, he fisted the hand braced on the side of her SUV and held up the note with his other. "Did you tell your father about this? Or any of what's been going on?"

"Not yet." She grimaced and reluctantly admitted, "Prior to last night, it was all just kinda random stuff. Nothing seemed connected."

"And yet you were still feeling paranoid."

She shrugged. "I was hoping I was overreacting. That it would just go away."

"Geezus fuck, Shelby." He thumped his fist against her car. "Now *that's* stupid."

Reyes shot him a frown. "Ease up, man."

He arched his eyebrows at his brother. "The fucking line was cut and you say *ease up*? She's lucky it wasn't her brakes."

Her stomach churned as she nodded. "I'll tell my dad today."

"*Now*." Dev gripped her elbow and steered her toward the door leading into the mansion. "You will tell him right now."

Shock delayed her response for a few steps, but then she jerked her arm free from his hand. "I said I'd tell him. I don't need you to march me inside like I'm a five-year-old."

He whirled around to face her. His expression pinched in pain for a second, then turned to stone. "You're acting like a five-year-old by thinking ignoring this will make it go away. That's a good way to get yourself killed."

The leashed anger in his voice sent her back a step as much as his blunt words. If she didn't know better, she'd think he cared, but no way that was true.

"That's a little extreme," she whispered.

He raised the fisted note between them once more. "*This* is extreme. Your parents have bodyguards, don't they?"

She drew back with a slight frown. "Of course. Dad gets death threats. Especially whenever someone doesn't like the way he votes on a bill."

"In this context, the word *death* is definitely a threat."

She reached up and snatched the note from his grasp. He was right, but it galled her to have him point out how willfully naive she'd been.

He continued to the door and held it open. "Are you coming with me, or am I telling your father about this by myself?"

She glanced at Reyes, but he was no help as he leaned against her vehicle, arms crossed over his chest as he watched the both of them with curious interest. Shelby turned back to Dev and held his gaze as she approached. Instead of passing through the door, she tipped her head up while slipping the wrinkled note into her back pocket. "Why are you making this your business?"

Surprise flashed in his eyes before he stiffened and looked away, denying her the chance to read anything else.

"You need to be protected."

The rough tone of his voice stirred butterflies in the pit of her stomach. "Are you volunteering?"

His gaze cut back to hers. "Fuck no."

And just like that, she was sixteen again, faced with Devante Torrez's brutal rejection.

Shelby stuffed her hurt deep down inside, stiffened her spine, and angled her shoulders to march past without touching him. She stripped off her coat along the way, and halted at the dining room entrance where everyone was gathered at the huge table loaded with food. Well, almost everyone. Asher and Honor had just gotten home from the hospital with Ava, so they were absent, and as usual, so was Grayson.

She almost kinda wished she'd skipped today.

No, Dev's right. I can't ignore this anymore.

His shoulder bumped hers as he stopped behind her. She shifted away at the same moment Celia looked up. Her older sister's eyebrows rose for a brief moment at the sight of her self-appointed escort, but then she waved them forward because there were plenty of times when they were younger when the Torrez kids had eaten with their family.

"Get in here you two. Sit down so we can finally eat."

"Everyone's waiting," Shelby said in a low undertone to Dev. "I'll tell him after brunch."

"Mr. Diamond." His voice projected over the noise, drawing the attention of the entire table. "I'm sorry to interrupt, but may I speak with you?"

Gritting her teeth in annoyance as everyone stared at them, Shelby said, "We. Can *we* speak with both you and Mom?"

Her father set his coffee cup down with a slight frown. "Can't it wait?"

"No sir," Dev insisted.

Her mom twisted in her chair, concern in her eyes. "Is everything okay?"

Shelby heard Dev draw a breath to speak and jabbed an elbow into his ribs to shut him up. At the same time, she heard Merit joke to Loyal, "Hundred bucks says she's pregnant."

Dev muttered behind her as she swung her narrowed gaze to her idiot grinning brothers. "I am not pregnant."

Gotta have sex for that.

Mae smacked her husband on the shoulder, and Merit rubbed the spot as he laughed.

Looking back at her parents, Shelby said, "I just need a few minutes, please. In your study, Dad?"

Curiosity lit his brown eyes as he nodded. "We'll be right there."

When she spun and pushed past Dev, voices erupted behind her. After Merit's joke, they'd probably dream up all kinds of scenarios. She could've just as easily told them all right there, but then she'd have like fifteen different people showering her with concern and advice and it was suffocating just thinking about it.

Dev followed, and as she reached the study, Shelby whirled to block the entrance. He jerked to a halt and reached out to grab the doorjamb with a wince.

She ignored a flash of sympathy—because God forbid she feel sorry for his pain—and demanded, "Why are you still here?"

"I was wrong earlier."

Wow. Hell must've frozen over. "About what?"

"You being level-headed."

That explained why he'd admit to being wrong—it had been something good about *her*.

"Experience proves you have a proclivity for doing rash, reckless things that put you in danger, so I'm making sure you tell your dad everything he needs to know."

Shelby scoffed. "A *proclivity*?"

"It means—"

"I know what it means," she snapped as she pivoted and strode into the room, tossing her coat over a chair on the way. "After nine years of being gone, Dev, you don't know *anything* about me."

"True, but that only proves my point."

The plush carpet had muffled his footsteps, and she stiffened at the unexpected nearness of his voice behind her. "How so?"

"The last time I saw you nine years ago, you offered yourself to me on a silver platter."

Her cheeks burned in mortification that he would throw that out there.

Coming up to her dad's desk, she forced herself to turn around and face Dev while leaning her butt against the edge. She refused to act like a broken-hearted teenager who was ashamed of what she'd done. "I was on my bed, not a platter."

A muscle ticked in his jaw. "Might as well have been."

He was still angry about that day. She hadn't understood his anger then or now. However, she understood hers over his ridiculous Neanderthal act.

Bracing her hands on the edge of the desk, she forced a small smile as her pulse picked up speed. "I assure you, it wasn't quite so rash and reckless as you might think."

"The hell it wasn't."

"But, Dev, you were just my practice run."

His dark eyebrows slammed together. "Your what?"

"My practice run," she repeated, lying through her teeth. "And thank goodness I got things right the second time, because the man I really wanted was more than up for the task." She tilted her head and added some sugar to her smile.

Judging by his clenched fists and the fire flashing in his dark gaze, he had no trouble figuring out what she meant. If the idiot wasn't so damn wound up, he'd see right through her lies.

"All right, what's going on?"

Her dad's firm voice from the doorway made Shelby jump a good inch. As he and her mom entered the study, she prayed they hadn't heard her last words. A quick glance eased that worry, and she met Dev's hard gaze before stepping past him while pulling the note from her back pocket.

"I think I have a stalker."

CHAPTER 5

*D*ev listened while Shelby explained to her parents what had been happening. He interjected when he felt she was downplaying—much to her irritation—but he wasn't about to let anything get in the way of her safety.

The entire time, the words *practice run* and *man I really wanted* kept popping into his head with infuriating frequency. On the one hand they made him want to punch a wall. On the other, he thanked God he hadn't done anything stupid all those years ago.

Like fall in love with her.

He stiffened at that thought and forced his head back to the conversation. Mark and Janine were both insisting on Shelby having a full-time bodyguard, and Dev was totally on board with that. It was precisely the reason he'd insisted she tell her father right away.

"Looking back, this could be tied to the vandalism at your clinic," her father said.

"That was months ago." She frowned. "And nothing's happened there since then."

"Because you halted construction," he argued. "Aren't you planning to start up again?"

"Mae's got me on the schedule for end of February, a week after Loyal and Roxanna's wedding."

"Then we'll add security there, too," Mark stated.

He glanced at Dev as if asking his opinion, and he gave the senator a nod of agreement while shifting to ease the ache in his leg.

Shelby didn't appear happy, but she grudgingly agreed, until the person behind the note was caught and dealt with, she'd have a bodyguard for protection.

"Then it's settled." Janine rose from one of the chairs in front of the desk. "Your dad will get things rolling after brunch, but for now, let's go eat. You'll join us, won't you, Dev?"

He straightened from his spot near the window as Shelby rose from her chair. Her glare in his direction made him want to stay just to spite her. "Thank you, but Reyes and I are on our way out for a couple days of camping."

"In the winter?"

He shrugged. "Just getting away for a bit."

Mental therapy for the both of them.

"All right then." She paused to give him a hug, which he returned with affection as she whispered, "Thank you for taking care of our baby girl."

Baby girl. Keep that in mind when you're thinking about how good her ass looks when she bends over.

Heat climbed his neck as he stepped back with an uncomfortable nod for her mother.

"If you don't mind, Devante, I'd like a word before you go."

The senator's request stopped him mid-turn for the door. He did mind. Now that Shelby would have the protection she needed, he wanted the hell out of there. Instead, he forced a polite smile. "Of course, sir."

"It's Mark." The senator crossed his arms with a grin as Janine left the room. "We covered this years ago, did we not?"

"Yes sir. Mark." Dev smiled, though it felt more like a grimace. "Sorry, sir, force of habit."

Mark chuckled. "After twelve years of service, I imagine it is."

Shelby made a sound of impatience from her spot in front of the chair. "What else is there to talk about, Dad?"

"You can go." He waved her after her mother. "I didn't ask you to stay."

"Is it about me?"

He hesitated, glancing between the two of them before saying, "I was going to offer Devante the job."

"Dev?" She immediately shook her head, her dark hair swaying from her vigor. "Uh-uh. No way."

He whole-heartedly agreed. "I'm sorry, sir—Mark— but that won't be possible."

The senator got up from his desk and moved around to lean against the front in the same way his daughter had earlier. "Why not?"

"Because he can't, Dad. Let it go," Shelby insisted.

His gaze bored into Dev's. "I know you're not working yet. Name your price."

The challenge had him gritting his teeth as he shot a glance at Shelby. Forget the temptation she provided—

because despite their animosity, he wanted her as much now as he had nine years ago. Forget the animosity, too, because that didn't matter any more than the money did.

But his pride...that was a whole other matter. And he'd be damned if he'd admit in front of Shelby the bitter truth that had resulted in his forced discharge from the military.

He wasn't physically capable of protecting her.

The throb in his leg underscored that fact—as did him wishing for his damned cane to lean on.

Having the truth shoved in his face stirred up his anger all over again. At life, the senator, Shelby—and most especially the worthless bastard threatening her safety.

Years of discipline training allowed him to say calmly, "This has nothing to do with money. I'm simply not interested."

Shelby dipped her head to frown at her feet. When he noticed her nip her lower lip between her teeth, a swift spike of longing made his breath hitch.

"Go ahead and get some breakfast, Bells. I want to talk to Dev alone." Her gaze jerked up to her dad's, and he offered a firm, "Please."

With another parting glare for Dev—a clear warning to not change his answer—she left the room, and he faced her father.

"I want you for this job," Mark stated. "I trust you."

Dev shook his head. The senator's trust didn't matter one bit when he didn't trust himself. "Get one of the guys from your detail for her. You trust them for you and Janine. They'll keep Shelby safe, too."

Mark held his gaze for a long moment, then released a

heavy sigh as he straightened and uncrossed his arms. "I can't really argue that, can I?"

"No, sir. And I'm sorry, but I really should be going." *Before I do something stupid like reconsider.* "Reyes is waiting."

The senator nodded and extended his hand. "In that case, I will add my thanks to Janine's. I appreciate you making sure we heard about this. Shelby can be a bit too stubborn for her own good sometimes."

Dev smiled his agreement as he shook the senator's hand before limping for the door. Sure the man's gaze watched his every step, his ears burned in mortification long after he moved out of sight. Mark was sure to be glad he'd refused the job.

He found Reyes waiting in the foyer with a large plastic baggie of cookies in hand.

"I loaded up my stuff and drove your truck up front."

"Good. Let's get outta here."

They were a few miles down the road before Rey broke the silence in the cab. "You gonna tell me what the hell that was back there?"

Dev kept his gaze trained on the road and tried to play it off. "What?"

"The whole Tarzan act with Shelby."

He scoffed. "It wasn't like that at all. I just want to make sure she stays safe, that's all."

"Riiight. "

"Man, shut up."

He caught Reyes' grin from the corner of his eye, but thankfully his brother dropped the subject.

They reached the trailhead a half-hour later, and loaded up with their gear for the couple mile hike to the campsite. Dev had purposefully chosen their location for the more level terrain so he wouldn't strain his leg too much. The exercise was good, but only if he didn't push too hard.

So, what the fuck did he do? Pushed too damn hard and ended up paying for it when his muscles seized in the middle of setting up their tent. He turned to brace a hand against a tree trunk, cursing under his breath while rubbing the heel of his hand over the spasm in his thigh.

Reyes came around the other side of the tent. "You okay?"

"Fuckin' peachy."

"Well, you're the one who practically ran all the way here. I don't know what the hell you're trying to prove."

He hung his head and dug harder into the tight muscles. "Mark offered me a job."

"Okay?"

"As Shelby's bodyguard."

"And?"

"And what?" he bit out. "I said no."

"Why? You said last week you weren't sure what you were going to do now that you're out. It's as good a job as any, and Mark pays well."

Dev whirled around and nearly fell when pain shot through his leg. "Does it look like I can fucking protect anyone like this?"

Seriously. What the hell was her father thinking? What the hell was he thinking that he wanted to?

Reyes shrugged and went to pick up the tent pole Dev had dropped when the spasm hit. "You should do it."

"Look at me." Hearing the self-pity in his own voice, he was thankful when his brother kept working on the tent.

"You know, half of the deterrent is you being there. It's like having a dog to protect against break-ins. Most times, it doesn't matter how big or small, as long as it barks."

Dev leaned against the tree as his massage began to ease the pain some. "By that logic, she should just get herself a dog." A big one.

Reyes grinned. "But your bark is already so very loud."

"Fuck you."

His brother laughed and Dev rolled his eyes as he limped over to resume helping. Sure, simply having him at her side would be a deterrent. But if something serious happened and she got hurt because he failed to protect her, he'd never be able to live with himself. He needed to leave that job to someone of sound mind *and* body.

He didn't qualify for the latter, and some days, he wasn't so sure about the former, either.

CHAPTER 6

A half-hour before three p.m., Shelby gave a perfunctory knock at the bridal suite before swishing the skirt of her floor-length, silver velvet dress inside and shutting the door. She'd left Celia, Honor, and Mae in the room next door, so she knew she'd have her soon-to-be sister-in-law to herself for a moment. Likely a very brief moment with the way wedding planner Maria was barking out orders.

Roxanna's gaze flicked to hers in the mirror before she returned her attention to the mascara wand for one last swipe over her lashes. A few pearl-studded pins held a wreath of white baby's breath and tiny copper-colored tea roses in her hair, but otherwise, her long brunette curls cascaded down the back of her ivory bridal gown.

Whereas the bridesmaids were all tricked out in cool silvers for the February winter wedding, copper and bronze shimmered on the bride's eyelids, and her brown eyes were framed beautifully by her long, thick lashes. Her cheeks glowed with happiness as she capped the mascara and set it down for one final look in the mirror.

"You look amazing," Shelby said with a grin.

"Thanks." She gave a bit of a wistful smile. "I can't believe after all the crazy of the past few weeks it'll be over in a few hours."

"Not over." Meeting her gaze in the mirror, Shelby leaned down to hug her shoulders. "Just on to the next chapter."

"I know. I meant the wedding, though." Now her smile turned wry. "So much for small and intimate."

"Come on, you knew this would happen even without being psychic."

"Your mom *is* hard to stop once she gets started."

"Consider yourself lucky. One hundred guests is better than Celia's five hundred."

"One hundred and two—but at least I actually know everyone." She tilted her head and squinted at the ceiling. "I think."

Shelby laughed as Roxanna swiveled around and took hold of her hands. "How are you doing? With everything going on, I feel bad I haven't been able to talk to you much since that day Devante showed up at brunch with you."

"Don't worry about it," she assured her, shifting sideways to drop down onto a chair. "I'm fine. And nothing's happened since then, so the whole bodyguard thing is beginning to feel a little melodramatic."

Like everyone's reaction at the brunch table three weeks ago when Dad had insisted they all know what was going on so they could be extra careful, too. She completely agreed on that, but the smothering had been even worse than she'd imagined.

"After what happened with your car, and the clinic last fall, it's *good* nothing more has happened," Roxanna said.

Looking at it all together, Shelby couldn't disagree. The extensive vandalism at her veterinary clinic had forced her to postpone construction back in October, and then Mae's early labor had extended the delay.

"Of course," she replied to Rox. "It's just that I hate not knowing how long this is going to go on. Having someone watching every move I make is uncomfortable, even though I know they're there to protect me."

"Your dad hasn't found out anything yet on who's behind everything? The cops got nothing from the flowers or the note?"

Shelby shook her head with a heavy sigh. "Nope."

Roxanna gave her a sympathetic smile and reached to squeeze her hand again. "Well, be patient. It'll all work out the way it should."

The way it should?

Shelby raised her eyebrows at the odd phrasing, but before she could ask if patience was a professional psychic recommendation, or if she was just voicing platitudes, the wedding planner breezed in with her clipboard.

Her future sister-in-law glanced at the buttoned-up, blond tornado talking a mile a minute into her headset, then leaned forward to whisper, "Can you do me a favor?"

"Of course."

"I had planned to message Loyal this morning, but Maria confiscated my phone last night. Will you go find Loyal and tell him I love him?"

"Aw, that's sweet, but you'll be telling him yourself in a half-hour."

Maria abruptly swung back toward the door. "I swear,

he's completely incompetent. I'll be right there." She pointed at the bride on her way out. "Twenty minutes to go-time. Do *not* leave this room."

Roxanna turned pleading eyes to Shelby.

A laugh bubbled up as she rose to her feet. "Okay, okay, I'm going."

She passed her fellow bridesmaids while following Maria out, then started across the church foyer to the opposite side where her brothers had been banished two hours earlier. She noticed her bodyguard near the main doors, chatting up her cousins from Texas and Washington D.C.

Blake didn't even glance her way, though with Raine's dark Diamond beauty, and Noelle's blond bombshell looks from her mother, it was no wonder his focus was concentrated elsewhere. It was kind of nice to have the break, and with all her family around in the church, she wasn't worried. She'd have even been fine giving him the day off.

In front of her, the wedding planner glanced back over her shoulder, and when she saw Shelby, she did an abrupt about face. "Where do you think you're going?"

One of her silver heels slid on the tile floor as she pulled up short while scrambling for an answer. "To pee." She arched her brows. "Or am I not allowed a potty break before the ceremony?"

Maria's gaze narrowed as she pointed in the direction they'd just come. "The bathrooms are over there."

Shelby pointed in the direction she was headed. "There are some over there, too."

"Make it snappy," the blond ordered before pivoting to head down the center aisle of the church.

She gave a mocking salute to the woman's back, then rolled her eyes as she dropped her arm and turned to go find Loyal. Her gaze collided with Dev's where he stood at the back of the church with his parents, and his sister, Solana.

Embarrassment burned her cheeks at the possibility of him having heard her saying she needed a potty break. Her breath caught when she saw what looked like a smile tugging at the corners of his mouth. Freshly shaved and sporting a recent haircut above the navy blue suit that fit his broad shoulders perfectly, the striking Torrez good looks were on full display.

"Hey, cuz—you look gorgeous."

Raine's voice drew Shelby around. After a quick hug, she shot Dev one last glance, but he was now walking with his family toward the front of the church. She couldn't help noticing the limp he seemed so self-conscious about—and the absence of his cane—*and* the absence of a date.

Nope, don't care.

She turned back to her cousin to find Raine watching the Torrezes, too. "Holy hotness. Is that Devante all grown up?"

"He was grown up the last time you saw him," Shelby pointed out.

"Yeah, but that was what, ten years ago?"

"Yep."

A year prior to her failed deflowering, when they were fifteen, Raine had been up for a summer visit when Dev was home on leave. The two of them had drooled over him at the pool most of the afternoon. He'd been twenty, tanned, muscled, and a military hero in their

44

young, romantic eyes, even though he had yet to be deployed.

Now he was thirty, still muscled, a seasoned Special Forces soldier, and a true military hero to her realistic eyes.

And also a Neanderthal jerk.

"Too bad he's got a date," Raine said.

"That's his sister, Solana."

Her cousin gave her a little nudge with her elbow. "That's good news."

Refusing to let her mind—or her heart—go down that road, she kept her lips zipped.

"Doesn't he have a brother, too?"

The question had Shelby biting back a grin. Raine didn't fool her with the innocent act. She knew damn well he had a brother. Because while they'd both voiced their teenage appreciation for Dev, her cousin had actually had a thing for the youngest Torrez, though she'd never openly admitted it. But she *had* flaunted her red bikini in front of Reyes every chance she got on that visit.

And last summer, when she'd been visiting after one of her equestrian events, Shelby was positive Raine had gone down to the barn with the excuse of going for a ride, but it had really been to try to get under Reyes' skin. Instead, he'd gotten under hers. Her cousin had been fuming when she'd joined her at the pool after her ride.

"Reyes is home sick, unfortunately," she informed Raine.

"Oh." A wealth of disappointment filled that one little word. Shelby wished he had been able to make it just so she could've watched the fireworks.

She did a quick scan to make sure Maria wasn't on the

warpath, saw Blake still distracted by Noelle, and lightly touched Raine's arm. "Come on, walk with me before the general comes back. How's your shoulder doing?"

She'd had surgery a month ago after a pretty serious accident during her final jumping event of the season.

"Good. I ditched the sling for the wedding."

"I noticed." As they walked, she glanced sideways at her cousin's plum sweater dress with lace detail down the length of the sleeves and across the neckline. "And love that dress by the way. You look great."

"Thanks."

"Have you started riding again?"

Raine shook her head. "Doctor won't clear me for a couple of weeks yet. I'm chomping at the bit, though."

"I bet."

They reached the groom's dressing room by then, and slipped inside to deliver Roxanna's message. Loyal was the most straight-laced one of the family, and seeing his happy smile made the assignment totally worth the trip. After quick hugs and well-wishes, Shelby hurried Raine back before Maria came looking for her. Her cousin broke away to join her parents and four brothers in the church, while she went to line up with the wedding party at the back for the start of the ceremony.

A half-hour later, while standing on the altar steps during the exchange of vows, she reflected on how much had changed over the past two years. Today was wedding number four for their family, and there were already two babies. Plus, she was pretty sure Loyal and Roxanna would be planning babies soon, and Celia and Robert had been trying to get pregnant for a few months already as well.

Which left her and their half-sibling, Grayson, still standing.

Still standing.

That thought brought a smile. Because, seeing the love shining in Loyal's eyes as he said, *"I do,"* she knew he was one hundred percent happy to have fallen. All of them were.

A tiny spurt of envy subdued her smile. While she still didn't know Grayson well enough to know how he felt about love and marriage, *she* wanted what her older siblings had.

Love.

A partner.

Babies.

It didn't have to be right away, but someday. Maybe soonish.

She glanced at her half-brother on the opposite side of the steps, who was practically the mirror image of the groom. Though he was only a groomsman, he looked more than a little claustrophobic in his tux, especially without his service dog, Remy, at his side. She definitely could not imagine him saying, "I do," anytime soon. Heck, she didn't think he was even dating anyone—and if he was, it clearly wasn't serious enough for that someone to be his plus one to the wedding.

However, if *she* was imagining a groom…

Shelby found her gaze on Dev at the end of the second row before she realized she'd even turned her head. Her heartbeat skipped hard. Damn it all anyway, he was still the man who came to mind when she pictured her own wedding day.

He appeared to be studying the stained glass

windows to his right, so she took a moment to study him. The past two times they'd met she'd been too emotionally keyed up to really get a chance to take him in.

Raine was right. The boy had become a man over the past ten years. Light from the window highlighted the angles of his face. The snowy-white of his shirt seemed to deepen his tan, though he'd always sported a little darker complexion thanks to his Spanish heritage. That same ancestry also blessed him and his siblings with model-like cheekbones, but they were sharper than she remembered. His whole expression was harder in a way that made her wonder what he'd all been through.

At most, he might have finger-combed the top of his dirty-blond hair, where he'd let his military cut grow out some compared to the short sides. The tousled look only accented his good-looks, especially with the slight beard shadow on his jaw adding a rugged edge that made her belly dip.

Abstractedly, she registered the pastor telling Loyal he could kiss the bride just as Dev started to turn his head back toward the couple. Shelby quickly averted her gaze, but not before she noticed Solana watching her watch her brother.

Heat warmed her face, and she had to fight the urge to fan her burning cheeks as the ceremony concluded.

Standing in the receiving line a few minutes later, her pulse kicked with stupid anticipation when she saw Solana and Dev's parents, Elena and Estefan. It slowed when she realized Dev wasn't with them. She didn't dare examine how she felt about him skipping, and then she forced herself to put him out of her mind as she rode with the wedding party in the limo over to The Piñon Hotel for the dinner reception.

Except, she couldn't help noticing his empty chair at dinner. It taunted her curiosity. Why was he not sitting with his parents and sister?

Why do you care?

After dinner was over and the music had started, she ventured out into the lobby to get a breath of fresh air near the doors. She hadn't quite realized how alone she'd been feeling lately. With the romance of the wedding, seeing Loyal and Roxanna so happy, and other couples in her family all lovey-dovey, it left her feeling a little melancholy.

Worse, it had her longing for her own romance and casting Dev in the role he'd turned down years ago. After how long it took for her to get over his rejection the last time, she knew her heart couldn't take another trip down that road with him.

Doesn't mean you can't make the journey with someone else.

For so long her focus had been on school, and then setting up her veterinary clinic. When that had been delayed, she'd thrown herself into her job at the animal hospital to get some experience under her belt. But clearly, there was so much more to life than working all day and going home to an empty apartment.

Restlessness had been building for a while, maybe even since Asher and Honor's wedding the previous May. Nine and a half months ago. Almost a year of her life had passed as she sat on the sidelines through two births and two—three weddings.

It was way past time to get herself out there and actively start dating.

With a bodyguard in tow?

Yeah. That'll be so *much fun. Not.*

"Shelby?"

She startled at the unexpected voice behind her, then forced a polite smile as she turned around to see one of the staffers from her father's senatorial campaign two years ago. "Hey, Chad."

"Hi. I thought that was you."

He was the one date she'd gone on in the past year. Well, kind of date. She'd only agreed out of obligation after he'd helped with some permit issues related to her veterinary clinic.

Because, though he was good-looking in a pretty-boy way with his blond hair and blue eyes, there wasn't anything about him that stirred her interest. If only he did. He was nice enough, extremely smart, and he had a good sense of humor. Most women would consider him a catch.

He moved in to give her a hug, and she stiffened against an instinctive reflex to step back. The smell of his cologne made her nose wrinkle. It had an odd feminine note to it, and she held her breath to keep from coughing when he held on a tad longer than was socially polite.

Lightly pushing free, she asked, "What are you doing here?" Because she knew he wasn't one of the hundred and two guests.

"Just hanging out with some buddies at the bar. You remember Jeff?" He gestured across the lobby to another of the guys from the campaign two years earlier. "He had a work thing down the road, so we stopped here after."

"Oh." The Piñon's upscale hotel lounge struck her as

an odd place to hang out, but what did she know? Her life had been school and work for the past eight years.

She took in his mussed blond hair and found herself thinking the style looked so much better on Dev.

Chad dipped his light blue gaze down and back up. "You're really dressed up."

"Loyal's wedding."

"Ah," he nodded. "You look beautiful."

"Thank you."

"Hey, you should come have a drink with us."

She forced her smile to stay in place, her cheeks about ready to cramp. "Thanks, but I should get back to the reception."

"Come on, just one drink," he coaxed with a smile. "Jeff wanted to say hi."

Then Jeff should've come over.

Surprised by the automatic retort, she bit her tongue to keep it inside. He was only being friendly. He'd only ever been friendly, even when they'd gone on their kind-of date last summer.

He reached for her arm, and she couldn't help an involuntary flinch from his touch. His brow pinched, eyes narrowing in a way that turned her stomach queasy. She took a step back, only to come up against a warm wall at the same time a deep voice sounded in her ear.

"There you are, Bells."

Shelby froze at the voice, the nickname, and Dev's thick forearm sliding around her waist while his breath stirred the loose curls softening her up-do. He'd stopped calling her Bells back about the time she turned thirteen.

"I've been looking all over for you."

He had?

51

She glanced over her shoulder in shock—and the sight of Dev's stony expression belied his husky, intimate tone. His narrowed gaze didn't waver from the man opposite them. When she turned back to face Chad's polite smile, confusion kept her tongue-tied.

"Excuse us." Dev's voice rumbled near her ear again. "They're playing our song."

What. The. Hell?

He made no move to lead her back to the ballroom, and when Chad gave a slight submissive nod of his head, it suddenly dawned on her what Dev had done. He'd come to rescue her. She was oddly relieved and offended at the same time. The warring emotions piled on top of her confusion.

"It was good to see you, Shelby," Chad said. "Tell Loyal I said congratulations."

"Yeah," she murmured. "I will."

As he left, her entire being focused on the muscled chest pressed against the bare skin of her back where her bridesmaid's dress draped down to her waist. Dev's body heat seeped through the velvet material covering her butt, making her heart race as she struggled to draw an even breath.

The first one she did manage to suck into her tight lungs had her closing her eyes in defeat. Of course *he* would smell divine. Strong and crisp, with a woodsy hint of outdoors mixed with citrus, there was nothing remotely feminine about the manly scent seducing her senses now.

Before she could do something stupid like lean back against him, or stupider yet like turn into his arms, he slid his hand from around her waist to the small of her back and urged her ahead of him.

Insistently.

Jolted by the juxtaposition of his gentlemanly rescue followed by him literally pushing her along, she frowned and took a breath to protest, but his voice growled in her ear.

"Where the hell is your bodyguard?"

CHAPTER 7

$\mathcal{D}$ ev nearly ran Shelby over when she put on the brakes.

"How am I supposed to know?"

Her annoyed retort spiked his anger enough to override the swift stab of pain in his thigh and knee at their abrupt halt. If she didn't know where the guy was, she should know better than to go out into the lobby with no one to watch over her. "Damn it, Shelby."

Jaw clenched, he gripped her elbow and propelled her forward once more. At the ballroom doors, she jerked her arm free and turned left to stalk down the hall, toward the hotel guest rooms. He followed at a slower pace to ease the ache in his leg.

"I'm not sure you understand how this works," she said while pivoting to face him with a defiant tilt of her chin. "He's paid to know where I am, not the other way around."

He wished he could argue that, but she was right. "How often does this guy not know where you are?"

"How do you know he's not watching right now?"

"Because if he was, he wouldn't have let that guy in the lobby get within five feet of you. And he damn well shouldn't have let me lay a hand on you."

"So you *do* know you're acting like a jerk," she snapped.

Dev ignored that as he glanced farther down the hall, toward where the guest rooms started around the corner, about ten feet away. "I also saw him disappear a good fifteen minutes ago with that blond he was chatting up at the church."

Her eyebrows rose as she looked in the same direction. "Noelle?"

Distracted by the soft, dark curls accentuating the graceful line of her neck, he muttered, "Whatever her name is."

"That's my cousin."

That kind of rang a bell. "Of the D.C. Diamonds?"

"Yeah."

He remembered how she and her brothers and sister used to joke about the D.C. Diamonds, the Dallas Diamonds, and the Denver Diamonds. They'd always seemed closer to the cousins in Dallas than in D.C.

A slight frown dipped her eyebrows as she continued to stare down the hall. Even with a frown, she was beautiful enough to steal his breath away. At the church, he'd had to force his gaze to the stained glass windows when he noticed his sister's too-perceptive FBI gaze shifting from him to the object of his attention for most of the ceremony.

For years, he'd only ever seen Shelby with her long, dark hair in a sleek ponytail. As a kid, and on through her teens.

But tonight, she was all woman—a fact that had slammed home when he'd slid his arm around her waist back there in the lobby. If he hadn't been so focused on running Chad off, the feel of her lush body combined with the light, summery notes of her perfume would've had him hard in seconds.

With the formal elegance of her upswept hair, a rich burgundy gloss staining her lips, and the way her shimmery velvet dress clung to her breasts and hips, she was classy and sexy. The seductive drape of velvet below her bare back got a man thinking about the fact she wasn't wearing a bra as his gaze traced the line of her exposed spine, down to her perfectly shaped ass.

How easy it would be to slip a hand inside the back of that dress and skim around to the front, sliding up over her ribs until he could cup the weight of her breast in his palm. If her nipple wasn't hard already, a teasing brush or two of his thumb would do the trick—

The rush of blood to his groin had him jerking his thoughts back to reality at the same time Shelby faced him again.

Desperate to redirect his thoughts, he moved past her to look around the corner of the hall. Closing his eyes briefly against the scent of jasmine that teased his senses, he steeled his resolve and turned back to ask, "Who was that guy in the lobby? Do you know him?"

She flicked her gaze in the direction they'd come from a few minutes earlier. "Chad Mayer. I worked with him on my dad's campaign a couple years ago."

"I didn't notice him at the church."

"Well, no, because he wasn't invited."

Explained why he was dressed a hell of a lot more

casual than the rest of the wedding guests. "Then what's he doing here?"

"He was with friends at the bar."

Disbelief arched his eyebrows. "In *this* hotel?" Where the drinks were at least double what they'd pay at a club?

"He said one of the guys had a work thing nearby, so they came here after."

"Do you actually believe that?" Because there wasn't a snowball's chance in hell he did.

Her gaze wavered in a moment of hesitation. "I have no reason not to."

"How well do you know him?"

She shrugged, looking slightly uncomfortable. "We hung out some during the campaign, and went to dinner this past summer after he helped me with some permit issues for my veterinary clinic."

The thought of her on a date with that guy made his gut twist.

You've got no fucking say who she dates.

He switched his focus to her reaction in the lobby. "Why don't you like him?"

A slight frown dipped her eyebrows. "What makes you think I don't like him?"

"Your face when you first saw him. The way you kept easing away." Not to mention her swift jerk backward when the guy had reached for her arm.

Speculation filled her brown eyes as she raised her gaze, and he realized what he'd revealed by letting her know how close he'd been watching.

"You shouldn't have been out there alone," he said to redirect her attention.

"I have tons of family around," she protested. "It's not like I'm in any danger with this many people here."

He shook his head at her naiveté. "Your guard is completely down, Shelby. With the wedding and all the drinking, it's a perfect opportunity for someone to make a move."

Someone like that Chad guy. From the moment he'd seen him watching her, Dev's radar had been pinging like crazy. Maybe his buddy had had a work thing, but unless they were trust-fund kids, The Piñon Hotel was not a place guys in their mid-twenties would choose to hang out. Hell, even if they had millions burning a hole in their pockets, it still wasn't the place to knock back a couple of beers after work. Unless you'd just completed a multi-million dollar real-estate deal. Or stock trade. Or some shit like that.

Shelby crossed her arms over her stomach, her expression now haunted. "God, I hate this. The police can't do anything, and Dad's private investigator hasn't turned up anything in the past couple of weeks. And what happens if he doesn't? How long am I supposed to live with a shadow? How long am I supposed to look over my shoulder, jumping at every little thing?"

Though he hated the anxiety and unhappiness in her voice, he didn't sugarcoat his answer. "As long as it takes to make sure you're safe."

She turned away with a shake of her head, then swung back to challenge, "And what do you care, Dev?"

He gave a slight shrug. "We pretty much grew up together, Shelby. Of course I'd never want to see you get hurt."

"Then I guess it's a good thing you walked out of my bedroom that day, isn't it?"

He stiffened at the not-so-subtle confirmation he'd hurt her. "I did that for your own good."

"You're such a hero. Because every sixteen-year-old girl needs a good dose of humiliation to help her grow up." Before he could respond, her attention shifted past him and she lifted her chin. "Since you're all about what's good for me, you can go now. Blake's back."

Dev twisted around to see the bodyguard had just rounded the corner. The guy was in the middle of tucking in his shirt under his suit coat. His step hitched when he spotted them in the hall, but then he straightened, ran a hand through his dark hair, and gave a tug on the sleeves of his coat while puffing out his chest.

"This guy bothering you, Ms. Diamond?"

Dev stepped between them. "Don't even bother, buddy. You're fired."

Blake halted, his head doing a comical little surprised jerk. "For what?"

"Fucking around on the job. Literally."

"Dev," Shelby protested.

The guy's cheeks flushed even as he scoffed. "You can't fire me."

Shelby's blond cousin strolled around the corner. She tossed her long locks over her shoulder and put a little extra sway in her hips as she sauntered past with a grin for the bodyguard. Then she shot her cousin a smirk. "Thanks for the borrow, Bells."

Dev arched his brows at Blake. "You want to explain that one to Senator Diamond or are you just gonna go?"

The guy clenched his jaw and strode forward to

shoulder past with a hard jolt to Dev's. A quick step back to keep his balance had him fighting a wince, even as he was relieved that was the extent of the confrontation when the jerk headed for the lobby exit.

Though the guy had a good half-inch on him and a solid build that would make most guys think twice, three months ago Dev would've taken him down without blinking an eye. Now, he was still dealing with the limitations of his injury, and hated to admit the bodyguard might have had a chance.

"That's just perfect, Dev. He picked me up this morning. How am I supposed to get home now?"

He turned to find Shelby glaring at him, head tilted, eyes narrowed, hip cocked. Her crossed arms pushed her breasts up to display a healthy dose of cleavage, and it took some effort to keep his gaze on her face.

"You don't have a room here for the night?"

She shook her head.

"Can't you go home with your parents?"

"I don't live with my parents. Besides, they're flying back to Washington after the wedding. Mom has a luncheon tomorrow she can't miss."

Great. Maybe he should've kept his mouth shut.

No. The fact that Blake hadn't even tried to apologize or plead his case to Shelby before bugging out more than confirmed he was a piss-poor bodyguard. Not to mention a poor excuse for a man.

Which now left Dev no choice but to step up.

"Fine. I'll take you home."

CHAPTER 8

*H*ands firmly planted on her cousin's waist as the rowdy dance line wound through the tables, Shelby swung her hips side to side while "The Locomotion" pulsed through the speakers.

After they passed where Dev was sitting, Raine turned her head to speak over her shoulder.

She leaned closer to hear over the music. "What?"

"I said, you should ask Devante to dance. He's been watching you all night."

Shelby snorted. "He's only watching because he got rid of my bodyguard."

"Why'd he do that?"

"He said he was doing a bad job." And technically he had been. But it hadn't been Mr. Neanderthal's place to make Blake leave.

"Interesting." Raine shot Dev another glance before the line wound the other direction.

"Annoying," Shelby corrected above the music.

"You should still ask him to dance. On the next slow song, of course."

Shelby shook her head. Giving Dev a chance to reject her in any shape or form wasn't going to happen ever again.

She resisted Raine's not so subtle nudges, and as the final song of the night faded a half-hour later, she exited the dance floor with the last of the guests who'd stayed after Loyal and Roxanna had said their thank yous and goodbyes. Other than her parents, the rest of her immediate family had gone home, but she purposely stayed to the very end just to spite Dev. Hell, she'd stay another hour if she could—and have another glass of champagne, even though she'd reached her limit one glass prior.

She wasn't drunk, but the alcohol helped ease her annoyance over Dev's overbearing attitude. The whole time she danced, she was acutely aware of his gaze watching every move from his table near the dance floor. The intensity of his blue-green eyes made her self-conscious and nervous, so she'd over-compensated with the champagne while shaking her ass every chance she got.

Now it was time to go home.

With him.

Her stomach flip-flopped at the thought of being alone with the sexy veteran for the ride home. And the walk to her door.

Oh stop. It's not like you're on a date and have to worry whether or not he's going to kiss you. Because you already know, he's not.

She hugged Raine and Noelle goodbye until the gift opening tomorrow, and her cousins headed toward the guest rooms arm in arm, heads together as they leaned on each other.

Dev rose and limped to her side. "You ready?"

She wished there was someone else she could chat with, but the room had mostly cleared out. Darn it. "I just have to get my coat."

When she angled past him for the coat room, a graze of fingertips at the small of her back made her pulse jerk. A moment later, the warmth of his touch disappeared, and he followed a few steps behind.

Had he touched her on purpose and then thought better of it? Or had it simply been an instinctive move—*a gentleman's move.*

She snorted under her breath. Dev had proved time and again he wasn't a gentleman.

Her dad was slipping her mom's coat over her shoulders when Shelby entered the alcove off the ballroom. Dev leaned a shoulder against the wall at the entrance.

"You guys off to the airport?" she asked.

"Yes," her mom confirmed with a tired smile. "Though, I would have much rather spent tomorrow here with all of you."

Sunday brunch would be extra full with aunts and uncles and cousins while her parents were dealing with politics in Washington. Despite the inconvenience of this one time, she knew they both loved it.

Shelby pulled her knee-length, black wool coat from the hanger and slipped it on as she followed her parents out to the lobby. They made small talk with Dev for a moment before her dad gave the area around them a sweeping glance.

"Where's Blake?"

She offered a grim smile while knotting the belt of her coat with a firm tug. "Dev fired him."

His gaze swung to the man beside her, a frown darkening his face. She didn't feel the least bit bad for ratting him out—but then again, Dev didn't bat an eye at the displeased look her dad gave him.

"He let *you* fire him?"

"Tells you the kind of job he was doing," Dev stated.

Her dad's gaze narrowed. "Since you took it upon yourself to fire him, I expect you'll do better?"

"Yes sir."

Shelby stiffened as she glanced from one to the other. "*No*," she protested with an adamant shake of her head. "Dev's only driving me home tonight. You can hire someone else tomorrow."

Her father raised his arm to look at his watch. "It's already tomorrow. He's hired."

"Dad."

He raised his eyebrows at her one word protest, but before she could add more, her mom stepped forward to pull her into a hug. "I'm sorry, honey, but the plane's waiting. We trust Devante will do a good job."

Resentment bubbled inside as her dad gave her a hug and kiss next. Then he turned to extend a hand to her newly appointed bodyguard. "Call me later and we'll discuss the particulars."

Dev shook his hand with a curt nod.

Shelby held tight to the ends of her knotted belt, her jaw aching from her clenched teeth even as she noticed her dad do the whole hand at the small of her mom's back as they left the lobby.

On the way out to Dev's big, black pick-up truck, she

wished she'd have asked Raine if she could crash in her hotel room for the night. Then she could've called her dad in the morning to talk about getting a different bodyguard instead of being stuck with Dev.

He moved ahead to open the passenger door, and she gathered the long skirt of her dress so she could step onto the running board and pull herself up into the truck. As she settled in and turned to click the seatbelt in place, she spotted his cane leaning against the console on her side of the cab.

A quick glance caught him as he rounded the back on the driver's side. That hitch was there in his gait, same as it had been all evening. She didn't think he was any less of a man because of it, but God forbid she even glance below his waist.

He got in and secured his seatbelt before starting the engine. "What's your address?"

"What happened to your leg?"

His gaze jerked to hers, his surprise evident in the dim light from his dashboard. Yeah, she hadn't expected that blunt question either. But she brushed aside a twinge of guilt for asking. So what if her question didn't fall in line with polite etiquette? He'd bossed her around and made decisions about her life tonight without once asking her what she wanted.

Dev looked away, his fingers tightening on the steering wheel. "You don't think I can protect you?"

Under the tightness in his defensive voice, there was a hint of vulnerability she was sure he would not want her to identify. As if maybe he had his own doubts. *That* made her feel bad enough she had to bite her tongue on an apology. He'd always been confident, strong, and capable, and after nine years as a Special Forces soldier, it would take a lot more than a limp to make her doubt his ability to keep her safe.

"That's not what I asked."

He put the truck in gear and drove toward the parking lot exit. "Where do you live, Shelby?"

She didn't reply. Didn't plan to until he answered her first.

When he reached the road, he braked and waited as light snowflakes began to drift down and melt on the windshield. She crossed her arms and turned to watch his profile, determined to get one thing she wanted out of this night.

The moment the question had left her lips, she realized she badly wanted to know what had happened to him. Because while physically he was still the same strong guy she'd known all her life, he was different in a way she couldn't quite define. Harder? Distant? If she knew what had happened, maybe she could figure him out.

You don't need to figure him out. He doesn't want you—not before, not now. Let it go!

After another thirty seconds, Dev flipped on his left blinker and gave her one last glance. One last chance. She thought he was bluffing, but he stepped on the gas and pulled out onto the road in the opposite direction of her apartment complex.

She let out a little growl of annoyance. "Where are you going?"

"Home. I'm not gonna sit here all night because you're acting like a spoiled brat."

A spoiled brat?

Shelby glared out the window, balling her hands into

tight fists as she fought the urge to reach over and hit him. After another half-mile, she unclenched her jaw and rattled off her address.

He checked his mirrors before flipping a U-turn.

A few miles later, she grudgingly asked, "You know where it is?"

"I have a friend who lives near there. I've driven by a few times."

Girl *friend?*

Nope. Don't care, remember?

She remained silent until they reached her complex, then she gave him her private gate code, and directions to her building. He pulled up slowly, his gaze scanning the area as he parked outside her garage bay. When she reached for the door handle, he ordered, "Wait for me."

She paused in surprise. That was something Blake never did, though the one older gentleman who sometimes filled in on his days off usually did.

Dev came around to open her door and offered her a hand down. She hesitated, but didn't have much choice if she wanted to avoid tripping on her long skirt in her high heels. The moment his rough, warm fingers took hold of hers, a spark of electricity zinged up her arm. She sucked in a quick breath at the same moment his grip tightened.

Once her feet were on solid ground, he released her as if he didn't want to touch her any longer than absolutely necessary. He didn't speak on the way inside the building and down the hall to her door. His sharp gaze surveyed everything as if he were on a mission—at least she *assumed* he approached a mission with the same level of intense awareness.

His hyper-vigilance threw Blake's more casual

approach into stark contrast. The odd thing was, she wasn't sure if it heightened her anxiety, or made her feel more secure. Her stomach was a bit uneasy, but she guessed that was more from Dev's presence than anything else.

At the door, she said, "I'll need you to pick me up tomorrow—or later, today, actually, since it's almost one a.m. So, say around ten, for brunch and the gift opening at my parents' house. Then Loyal and Roxanna are leaving for their honeymoon after that."

Quit babbling!

"Fine."

"Great. Then I'll see you at ten." She turned to punch in her code for the keyless lock.

Dev's hand closed over hers on the handle, his chest brushing against her back as her pulse skipped like crazy.

"Does Blake not check your apartment when he brings you home?"

"No." Fighting to keep her breath even, she added, "He walks me to the door and makes sure I get in okay."

He muttered what sounded like *fucker* under his breath.

"It's fine, Dev. I make sure everything is locked up when I leave." And she always left the lights on so she wouldn't be freaked out walking through a dark apartment.

"I'm sure you do, but I'm still going to want to check for myself."

"You don't have to—"

"I do," he insisted. "And if you don't mind, I'd like to get home before two a.m."

Shelby pressed her lips together while re-keying in her

code. Here she was all wound up from his nearness, and he was right back to being a jerk.

She let him go inside first. As she closed the door, he strode from her foyer to the kitchen, to the living room, his gaze scanning every inch of her apartment. He even brushed aside her drawn curtains and shades to check each window lock along the way. She'd wonder what he thought of her place, but it was clear he wasn't really *looking* at anything beyond security.

After shrugging off her coat and hanging it in the closet by the door, she kicked off her heels and slid her feet into her favorite pair of fuzzy slippers. By then, Dev had moved into the bathroom, and she heard the shower curtain zip along the rod. He came back out to check the guest bedroom and a linen closet across the hall, then disappeared into her bedroom.

She cringed when she thought about the fact she hadn't made her bed or picked up her dirty clothes in a few days. However, it was better to think about that than the fact Devante Torrez was in her bedroom again after nine years.

Leaning one hip against the island counter, she reached up to start removing the silver pearl pins from her hair as she heard the shower curtain in her master bathroom. Wow. He was being awfully thorough.

When he strode down the hall toward her a minute later, she quipped, "Don't forget to check under the couch."

Annoyance tightened his features, and his gaze narrowed. "This isn't a fucking joke, Shelby. You're coming home with me right now."

CHAPTER 9

*F*ury roughened Dev's voice as adrenaline tensed every muscle in his body.

Shelby froze for a moment, then lifted her chin as she lowered her arms. "I'm not going anywhere with you. And I told you not to swear at me."

Half her ebony hair cascaded in loose curls over her shoulder, past the swell of her breast. Melting snow glinted in her hair from the light overhead. Dev knew he shouldn't be noticing how beautiful she was at a time like this, but the way the shimmery silver velvet of her dress contrasted with her dark hair and pale skin was stunning.

A flash vision of her mirror made his gut coil with another surge of rage.

"You'll change your mind once you see your bedroom."

His grim prediction subdued her defiance as color drained from her face. "What do you mean?"

He didn't want to force this on her, but it was the only way to impress upon her how fucking serious the whole thing was. "Come see."

Her gaze darted toward the hall and back to him as she slowly moved forward. Dev let her pass and then followed just behind her. She stopped two steps into the room, her gaze sweeping over the messy bed and clothes piled on the floor near the closet. He guessed she'd made that mess since she didn't react to it at all.

But then she turned toward her vanity, and he saw her body stiffen when she spotted the block lipstick writing on the large mirror.

BEAUTIFUL SILVER BELLS. CAN'T WAIT TO SEE YOU IN RED.

Her brown eyes went wide, and her hand flew to her mouth to smother a gasp. "Oh my God."

"Pack a bag. You're not staying here tonight."

She stared for a long moment, frozen in her spot. The muscles in her throat worked in an audible gulp as she glanced toward the windows. "I double checked everything was locked."

"It still is," he confirmed.

She shot him a frown, then turned back to look at the mirror. After a long moment, her expression twisted, and she strode toward the vanity, her dress swirling about her legs. Dev let her go—until she swiped a handful of tissues from the box on her end table.

"Whoa—what are you doing?" He surged forward to catch her raised arm before she reached the mirror.

"Getting rid of it."

She strained against his hold, and he wrapped both arms around her from behind, pulling her back against his chest to subdue her struggles.

"Let me go." Anger vibrated in the sharp demand. "I want it gone."

"You have to leave it for the cops, Shelby."

She shook her head wildly, strands of her hair catching on the stubble on his jaw. "I don't want to see proof that some pervert was in my apartment. In my *bedroom*." Her voice cracked at the end, and her breath caught on a sob.

When her body trembled against him, his chest tightened as if squeezed in a vice. He turned her around in his arms and held her close while smoothing a hand over her snow-damp hair. She sagged against him, arms sliding under his suit coat to wind around his waist and hold on tight.

"You're going to pack a bag and come home with me for now," he said firmly. "I'll call the police to check things out first thing in the morning."

"He was watching," she whispered, the words muffled against his shirt. "Whoever it was saw my dress and—"

"Shh."

"He knows my nickname."

Dev tightened his hold for a brief moment, then slid his hands to her bare shoulders to ease her back and see her face. The shimmer of moisture in her eyes had him steeling himself from pulling her close once more.

"I'm not going to let anything happen to you, okay?"

She swallowed hard, her brow furrowed as she nodded.

"Good. Let's get your stuff and go."

She gave him another nod while pulling her arms from around his waist. Her hand slid along the waistband of his dress pants, and all of a sudden her eyes widened as she jerked back a step. "Is that a gun?"

Knowing she'd felt the hard edge of his concealed

carry holster with his 9mm Beretta, his hand automatically went to the weapon. "I have a permit."

Her gaze rose to his. "Were you wearing that the whole day?"

"Yes."

"Why?"

"Never leave home without it." After twelve years in the military, it was as much a part of him as his legs and arms. She'd dropped her gaze once more, and he gave her another moment before wind-milling his hand at the wrist. "Can we get moving here?"

She blinked, and gave a quick shake of her head. "Yeah. Sorry. It just surprised me, that's all."

After one last glance at his waistline, she crossed the floor to her open closet.

"Only touch what you need to," he warned. "And use one of those tissues when you open your dresser drawers."

She nodded silently while stuffing clothes into an overnight bag. He noticed her hand pause mid-reach for a red sweatshirt, then jerk away to grab a gray zip-up hoodie. Then she moved to the dresser and pulled out underwear and a bra. He refused to look too close at the black scraps she fisted in her hand.

Realizing she'd stilled, he saw her gaze shifting around the room. It locked on the mirror as she murmured, "I can't think of what else I need to bring."

Dev moved in front of her to block the words. "Shoes. And a toothbrush. I don't think I have any extras."

"Right." She stuffed the underwear in her bag, added a pair of tennis shoes, and then made a quick detour to the bathroom. After she dumped a handful of items in her bag with her toothbrush, she zipped it shut. "That should be it."

"I'd say you could change out of your dress before we go, but—"

"No, I just want out of here."

Good. He hadn't wanted to creep her out more by pointing out her stalker could've planted a hidden camera. After the police did their work, he'd be doing his own thorough sweep for any electronic devices.

"All right, let's go." He reached past her to grab her bag and caught the subtle lingering scent of her perfume. Forcing himself to focus, he swung the duffle's strap over his shoulder and led the way out after she put her coat back on.

He didn't have to tell her to stay close on their way to his truck, she was practically glued to his side as she shuffled along in a pair of slippers peeking out from beneath her dress. Knowing she had the tennis shoes in her bag, he didn't bother pointing them out.

Dev tuned in to their surroundings, listening to his instincts, searching for that telltale prickle of hair on the back of his neck to signal danger in the dark. The whole world seemed muffled by the snowfall, and all remained quiet as they got in the truck. He lived about fifteen minutes away in a sprawling, wooded suburb, but he drove a meandering route that took closer to twenty-five minutes, keeping watch for any tailing headlights along the way.

Shelby kept busy dragging pins from her hair until the remainder of her curls pooled at her shoulders. She stuffed the pile of pins in her coat pocket and then sat silently, staring out the windshield.

When he was sure they weren't being followed, Dev shot a glance across the dim cab. "You doing okay?"

Her head jerked with a nod, but then she switched to a negative shake. He firmed his grip on the steering wheel to keep from reaching for the clenched fingers in her lap.

"I don't understand how someone got in when everything was locked." Her brow furrowed in the dim light from the dash. "Did they get a key somehow? Or know my code? Is it someone I know?"

The fear in her voice made him want to throttle the bastard. "Does anyone have your code? Or a key?"

"Other than my parents, no."

"Boyfriend?"

"No. I don't have a boyfriend."

Even though he'd figured she didn't since she hadn't brought a date to the wedding, the confirmation twinged an emotion he refused to acknowledge.

"What about a recent breakup? Or a bad one in the past?"

She merely shook her head through each question. He wanted to clarify, no breakups, or just no bad ones? But that would be a dumb question, wouldn't it? Of course she'd dated and had relationships. Beauty aside, she was sweet and fun and smart enough to make every conversation interesting. Or at least she had been at sixteen, which is what had made her offer back then so damn dangerous.

And maybe she was still all those things now. She'd been absolutely right a few weeks ago when she accused him of not knowing anything about her after the past nine years. Problem was, much as he hated to admit he wanted to know, he recognized the danger of getting too close to her was just as high now as it had been way back when.

His number one priority had to be protecting her from the sonofabitch turning her life upside down.

"We'll figure it out," he assured her while checking the mirrors to make the left turn onto his road. At nearly two a.m., there wasn't another car in sight and hadn't been for the past couple of miles. "The cops can talk to the super, and they'll look at video surveillance from the security gates to see who came and went after you left for the wedding. *And,* you know your dad will have his PI on this in a heartbeat."

"Yeah. Not that he's found anything yet."

He didn't reply to her subdued statement as he pulled into his driveway and parked outside the garage. He'd turned the space into a workshop when remodeling, but needed to build a detached shop in the spring before he could switch it back. Before his discharge, he'd never been home long enough to need inside parking for more than a couple of weeks.

He reached for his cane, though he hated to use it after Shelby had asked point-blank about his injury. Unfortunately, the fresh snow on his driveway made it a necessity after the long day.

As he rounded the back of his truck on her side, he lifted her bag from the back before continuing to the passenger door. She already had it open and was stepping off the running board when he reached her. Her feet slipped on the snow as she closed the door, and he snaked an arm out to catch her from going down.

Shelby grabbed his suit coat lapel, a surprised gasp parting her lips when her body slammed against his. Dev leaned hard on his cane to keep his balance as he held her tight against his side. When he straightened to steady her on her feet, she glanced up in the dim light cast from his front porch lamp.

His breath seized in his lungs, heart thudding hard against his ribs. Deep down in his gut, he knew he was screwed. Focusing on priority number one was going to be damn near impossible when all he wanted to do in this moment was lower his mouth to hers and beg her to let him change his answer to her offer nine years ago.

CHAPTER 10

$\mathcal{P}$ ushing away from Dev took willpower Shelby struggled to employ—especially when she dropped her gaze to his lips. The urge to rise up on her tiptoes and press her mouth to his battled her common sense. Her slippers would never lift her high enough. And if she slid again on the slick soles, she'd end up planting her lips on his chin or something equally humiliating.

Which is why you are not *going to kiss him.*

"You good?" he asked in a gruff voice.

"Yeah, thanks." She finally managed to put some space between them and looked at her feet with a self-conscious grin. "I didn't even think about my slippers until after we'd left my apartment. I should've changed them."

"I have hardwood floors. I'm sure you'll be glad you have them."

He abruptly continued toward his front door, and she followed with a wry twist of her lips. Leave it to Dev to put all the distance between them she needed.

78

Turning her attention to the small, plain ranch house, she asked, "Is this yours, or do you rent?"

"I bought it about eight years ago." He unlocked the door and held it open for her, then flipped on the lights. "I didn't want to always have to stay at my parents' house when I came home on leave. Plus, I figured it was an investment. The neighborhood was just starting to grow, and I pretty much gutted the place and redid everything whenever I could get back for a week or two."

Surprised at the bevy of volunteered information, she moved a few steps inside while untying and unbuttoning her coat. The foyer area opened up to a house much larger than its curbside appearance indicated. And she certainly hadn't expected it to be so nice. She ran her gaze around the open floor plan, impressed with his work on the trim, the warmth of his paint choices, and a really cool pallet wood accent wall adjacent from a fieldstone fireplace.

Yet, as professional as the remodel appeared, there were no furnishings beyond a couch, an end table and lamp, and two pictures on the mantle. The spot where she assumed a dining room table would go was empty, and there were only two barstool chairs at the large island separating the living room from what looked to be a state of the art kitchen.

Other than a large, flat-screen T.V., he had nothing on the walls, no area rugs on the beautiful hardwood floors, no curtains on the windows—though the ones facing the road did have shades.

She'd make a bet he didn't entertain much.

"You've done a great job," she said as he reached to take her coat and hung it on a row of hooks beside the door. "Though, your interior decorating is a little...minimalist."

He shrugged. "I don't need much. All my essentials fit in a go-bag. The rest is just stuff."

"A go-bag?"

"It's a military thing."

"Oh." She opened her mouth to ask more, but he was already walking toward a short hall she assumed led to the bedrooms.

"You can have my room, and I'll take the couch," he said over his shoulder.

She frowned. "You don't have a guest room?"

"I have three of them. I only have one bed."

Right. Because a second bed wouldn't fit in his go-bag. "I'll be fine on the couch."

"It's not up for discussion." He continued down the hall, his voice reaching back. "I'm just going to grab a T-shirt and shorts, and it's all yours."

She followed him past a bedroom that he'd turned into a home gym, and at the end of the hall was the master suite. Nerves halted her feet in the doorway. Looking around, she was reminded of a hotel room when you first check in. Neat. Clean. Impersonal.

Dev had tossed her bag on his bed and was hanging up his suit coat in the closet while toeing off his dress shoes. Those he placed precisely side by side, in between a pair of Army boots and running shoes.

When he started loosening his tie, she swallowed hard at what would come next—shirt or pants?

Heat bloomed in her cheeks. "I really would rather sleep on the couch."

He shot her an impatient look. "And I would rather have you in here with the door closed. Anyone comes in the front, they have to go through me first."

The blunt words reminded her of why she was in his bedroom in the first place, and her stomach flipped as her pulse skipped. She hadn't thought of his offer as anything other than him being polite.

"Don't worry," he added. "I just changed the sheets this morning."

"That's not it. I..." She gestured helplessly while he hung his tie on a hanger with a couple of others. "I feel bad kicking you out of your bed."

"It's fine." He closed the closet and crossed the room to his dresser. "What isn't fine is the fact we're still talking about this when it's already two o'clock in the morning."

She grit her teeth in frustration at his attitude, then decided it wasn't worth arguing about. If he wanted the couch, let him take the stupid couch. "Fine. Whatever."

As she started for the bed, he gave her a wide berth, T-shirt and shorts in hand. He tossed out a sarcastic, "You're welcome," before shutting the door with a sharp thud.

Shelby flipped her middle finger after him with a low growl. She hadn't even wanted his damn room, so where did he get off acting like she should be grateful he'd made such a huge sacrifice?

After a deep breath and slow count to three, she blew it back out again—along with some of her stress. The man might be hot as hell, but he was also a hell of a jerk when he wanted to be.

Turning back to the bed, she unzipped her bag and took out her things, only to realize she'd forgotten pajamas. And she'd been in such a hurry to get out of there, she'd only packed one shirt and jeans for tomorrow. She didn't really want to sleep in the clothes she was going to wear in the morning, she definitely wasn't going to sleep in her bridesmaid's dress, and underwear or birthday suit was not happening in Dev's bed.

She eyed his dresser, then crossed over to open the second drawer. It made a slight scratching noise in the quiet, and she cringed while pulling out a large tan T-shirt. Carefully closing that drawer, she opened the top one in search of shorts.

After holding up a pair of gym shorts that would need a belt to stay on her hips, she gingerly pulled out a pair of his black boxer briefs. They'd look ridiculous, but at least the stretchy material would stay on.

And they're better than tightie whities.

The thought made her snort with amusement, and she kept them as she closed the drawer.

Once she changed out of her dress into Dev's T-shirt and briefs, she hung the silver velvet gown in his closet next to his suit coat. The silver and navy looked good together. She trailed her fingers down the length of his coat sleeve, then snatched her hand away when she realized what she was doing.

You're being an idiot. Go to bed!

She took a few moments to wash off her make-up and brush her teeth in the master bathroom, then slid between the crisp, fresh-scented sheets. After clicking off the bedside lamp, she laid her head down on the pillow with an exhausted sigh. Willing her shoulders to relax, she linked her fingers together over her ribs.

And stared at the ceiling in the dark.

Turned her head to stare at the empty pillow beside her.

Stared at the ceiling again.

Being in Devante's bed was surreal. How many times

had she fantasized about this back in her late teens? Yes, even after his rejection.

Too many times.

He was quite the crabby jerk, and yet, back in her bedroom when she'd first read those horrible words on her mirror, he'd shown a glimpse of the kind, caring guy she remembered as a kid. The strength in his arms when he held her had given her a sense of security she hadn't felt even with a bodyguard the past few weeks. Whoever had written that creepy message couldn't get to her with Dev as her protector.

CAN'T WAIT TO SEE YOU IN RED.

The words flashed in her mind and sent a shiver down her spine. What did that mean even? She fisted her fingers in the comforter across her chest, dragging it up to her chin. Thirty heart-pounding seconds later, she scooted up and reached over to turn the light back on.

Immediately, she focused on the lamp's reflection in the window to the left of the bed.

Dev had said if someone tried to come in his front door, they'd have to go through him first. But her stalker wouldn't be that stupid. If he was resourceful enough to follow them here, he'd go around and come through the window—and with the light on, he could probably see into the room without her even knowing he was there.

Another reach for the lamp plunged the room into darkness.

Shelby grabbed the second pillow to hug against her chest while staring toward the window in the dark. Her elevated heartbeat shortened her breath as anxiety spiked.

Shit.

Tears pricked her eyes. She blinked them away with

impatience. She hated the thought this guy was winning—and yet there was no way she was going to get one wink of sleep while sitting here all freaked out about everything that had happened.

Worrying what *could* happen.

Throwing aside the covers, she jumped out of bed and hurried to the door. The hardwood floor was cold beneath her bare feet, but a prickle of fear along the back of her neck refused to let her turn around.

Three seconds later, she reached the living room. Recessed lighting from under the kitchen cabinets cast just enough light for her to see Dev jerk up from the couch.

He met her halfway across the floor. "What's the matter?"

His hushed, clipped tone indicated he was ready for action, not angry. At least, not yet.

"I, um…" Realizing she still clutched the extra pillow, she blurted, "You didn't take a pillow."

He frowned when she pushed it into his hands. "You came out here to give me a pillow?"

She shrugged and then sidled around him to sit on the couch.

"Shelby." His tone held a note of warning.

"I know—you've got the couch. I'm just…" She glanced up at him and then quickly looked away as she scooted back and drew her chilled feet up off the floor. Wrapping her arms around her legs, she whispered, "I can't shut my brain off."

Dev stood over her for a long moment, and a peek from under her lashes revealed his fingers fisted in the cushy pillow.

"What are you wearing?" he asked.

Guilt made her cringe. She reached for the blanket spilling over the edge of the couch and dragged it up to cover her legs. "I wasn't snooping, I swear. I forgot pajamas."

Finally, he heaved a sigh, tossed the pillow on the far side of the couch where his head had been, and moved to sit next to her.

But not too close, she noticed.

"Sorry," she said without looking at him.

"It's fine. I know you were shook up."

"I'm still shook up." She hugged her legs closer to her chest and rested her cheek on her knees. "I can't stop thinking about him being in my bedroom. And I keep seeing flashes of what he wrote. He didn't even touch me and I feel so...violated."

Dev's hand moved as if to reach out to her, but then he curled his fingers into a fist on his thigh and leaned against the back of the couch. She wanted to tell him *his* touch wouldn't bother her, but she didn't want to assume that's why he'd checked himself, so she kept quiet.

"No one's going to get near you," he promised. "I'll make sure of it."

She stared at the black nylon of the gym shorts he'd changed into. What had he done with his gun? Did he have a safe, or was it within reach? She hoped within reach. Because she wanted Dev to have his gun handy if the creep who'd been in her bedroom showed up here.

"What did he mean that he can't wait to see me in red?"

"Shelby, they're just words."

"But what do you think that meant?" She loosened her

hold on her legs and twisted slightly to search out his gaze. His profile was half-lit and half-shadows, but even then she saw his jaw clench as he shook his head.

"I will not let anyone hurt you," he vowed.

She had a guess as to what the guy meant, but was afraid to say it out loud. Dev avoiding the question only led weight to her frightening speculation.

"The best thing you can do is try to put it out of your mind and get some sleep."

She ducked her head against her knees again and pushed back into the couch, wanting it to swallow her up so he couldn't make her leave. "I keep imagining him coming through the bedroom window."

"All the windows are locked."

"So were mine."

Her words hung between them, and in the silence, she heard a clock ticking. She focused on the sound, trying to pinpoint where it was coming from.

Somewhere behind her.

A sigh bordering on a growl came from Dev's side of the couch. She scrunched her eyes tight against another annoying sting of tears and whispered, "I'm sorry."

"You don't have to apologize," he said roughly. "You didn't do anything wrong."

"And yet you're still mad."

"At the motherfucker messing with your life, not at you."

"Okay, good. You're a little scary when you're mad."

He scoffed. "It hasn't seemed to faze you one bit."

She laughed into the blanket, only to have tears choke her throat.

"Hey—"

"Don't. This isn't from you," she assured him as she tossed her hair back and blinked the moisture away. "I'm just feeling helpless and caged in, and I am *really* tired, but...I don't want to be alone." The moment the words were out, she cringed at what he might think she was asking and quickly added, "Can I just stay out here with you?"

"Both of us on the couch with a perfectly good bed in my room?"

Cheeks burning, she gave him a wry grin. "Given the past, I wasn't about to ask you to sleep in there with me."

His lips quirked in not quite a smile. "No. I suppose not." He looked left, hesitated, then reached out to grab the pillow and rest it against his thigh on her side. "Here. Lay down."

With her head practically in his lap? Nope. She leaned back into her corner. "I'm good here."

"I don't bite."

"No, duh, Dev. I just don't want to take the whole couch from you, too."

He slouched down into the cushions and leaned his head back with yet another all-suffering sigh. "I've slept in places that make this couch seem like a luxury feather bed. As long as you don't take another half-hour to argue a moot point with me, I'll be just fine."

His tone had her clenching her jaw. After one last moment of hesitation, she maneuvered to lie down. "It's really annoying when you do that," she muttered as she wiggled into a comfortable position.

He reached over her to pull the blanket up to her shoulders. "Do what?"

"Make it sound like I'm being unreasonable when I'm only trying to be considerate."

"Is that what I sound like?"

"You talk to me like I'm still a kid."

"It's more that I'm not used to anyone questioning everything I say."

She frowned, her gaze fixed on the dark fireplace across from the couch. "I don't."

He gave a short laugh. "You do."

"Well, sorry if I'm not used to having everything in my life controlled," she retorted.

But that wasn't completely true. Her parents—mainly her dad—had been overprotective enough to drive her crazy growing up. Being busy with vet school, she'd gone with the flow until after graduation. It wasn't until they'd pushed back on her location choice in a less affluent neighborhood for her vet clinic last summer that she'd finally found her voice.

Now there was no going back, no matter who was ordering her around.

"It's not about control," he explained. "On a mission, it's about keeping the guys on my team alive. Not following orders gets people hurt. Or killed."

Her impulse to point out she wasn't one of his military missions was quelled by the gruff emotion in his voice. She swallowed past a sudden tightness in her throat. "Is that how you were injured?"

Tension filled the ensuing silence, and she waited for him to snap it was none of her business.

"That's a story for another time," he finally said. "Go to sleep, Shelby. *Please.*"

Surprised he hadn't completely slammed that door in

her face, she squirmed a bit to get more comfortable. Sliding her hand under the pillow, her fingers brushed up against his thigh. He shifted his leg away, and even though she'd jerked back as well, her chest constricted. It was as if after that comforting hug at her apartment, he couldn't stand to touch her again.

She squeezed her eyes tight against the hurt, then lay there wide awake, wondering how in the world she was supposed to sleep when she was all too aware of every breath he took?

CHAPTER 11

$\mathcal{D}$ev blinked awake with the dim light of impending sunrise, his body stock-still as he catalogued his surroundings. All was quiet in the house, and Shelby slept soundly on the couch beside him. Or half on him. She'd stretched out, pushing the pillow, her head, and shoulders up onto his lap sometime during the past four hours.

He took in her wild cloud of dark hair, stark against the white pillow. His view of her profile was blocked by a thick curl left over from the wedding, with just the curve of her cheekbone and tip of her nose visible. His hand was about two inches from brushing it back before he caught the movement and withdrew.

Fuck. After having held her against him three times in the past twelve hours, reaching to touch her was becoming a nearly impossible instinct to fight. Seeing his T-shirt and briefs skimming her curves hadn't helped one damn bit.

But fight it he must—which meant getting his ass up and out of reach.

One shift of his left leg sent a sharp pain through the tight muscles. He breathed through it, stealthily maneuvering from beneath the pillow and retrieving his weapon from under the couch cushion without waking Shelby. Not only did she need more than four hours of sleep, but he needed to do his morning physical therapy. It was slowly getting better each day, but he still didn't want her to witness his discomfort as he worked the stiff muscles.

Socks kept his steps silent as he double checked the house perimeter before limping into the spare bedroom he'd set up as a gym. He left the door open in case Shelby woke up before he was done, though he wouldn't bet on her being up anytime soon with how tired she'd been.

Grim determination got him through the initial stretches and PT, before he switched gears for an upper body workout that got his blood pumping for the day. It was nearing seven-thirty when he reached to grasp the pull-up bar just as Shelby poked her head around the corner.

She leaned against the doorjamb, hugging the wall somewhat as she said, "Morning."

Dev dropped his arms to his sides. "Hey. I didn't expect you up yet."

"Clearly, you've been awake for a while."

He shrugged and swiped the towel off the bench next to where he'd laid his sidearm within easy reach. "Military hours. Did I wake you?"

She shook her head, her gaze focused on the gun. "I'm usually at work by now."

"On a Sunday?"

91

Her soft smile jolted right to his heart. "Well, no, not Sundays. Monday through Thursday I'm at the hospital by seven, and Fridays I spend the day at the veterans foundation Loyal and Grayson started. You've met Grayson, haven't you?"

He was the half-brother they'd found out about a couple years ago. "Not formally, but I saw him at the wedding."

"I can introduce you at brunch today." Her nose scrunched up a tiny bit. "*If* he bothers to come."

He wasn't going in with her, but he didn't tell her that just yet.

After wiping his face, Dev flipped one end of the towel over his shoulder and picked up his Beretta to head for the door. Shelby's hair tumbled in disarray past her shoulders, and a swift glance took in her slim, shapely legs and bare feet. The burgundy polish on her toes matched her short nails. She'd worn a similar shimmery shade on her lips for the wedding yesterday.

He shifted his gaze back up, struggling not to linger on the drape of cotton over her hips and breasts. She made his plain, desert tan T-shirt look like a million bucks. He had no doubt she'd make his bed look even better.

Do not go there.

"Since you're up, we should get moving," he said. "We can meet the police at your apartment before heading over to your parents' place."

A shadow flitted across her expression, but she nodded as he angled his body to avoid brushing against her when he passed. Her brow dipped into a frown as she replied, "I can be showered and ready in a half-hour."

Dev took his shower in five minutes—he cut it short

when he started imagining Shelby under the steamy spray in his master bath. He could still hear the water running after he stepped out of the shower in the guest bathroom, and hurried to dry and dress in a pair of jeans, white T-shirt, and a gray sweatshirt.

After securing his concealed carry holster, he called Jensen Brennan, a Special Forces buddy in the area who'd opened his own home security business when he'd retired three years ago.

Dev shot the rearview mirror another lingering glance a couple miles after leaving Shelby's apartment complex. They'd spent the past two hours with the cops, giving their statements while a couple of officers went over her apartment with a fine-tooth comb. Given the previous incidents, and Shelby's relationship to the senator, the officer in charge had been meticulous in her inspection.

No hidden cameras or other devices had been found, and she promised to call as soon as they'd had a chance to review the security gate surveillance footage. If they were lucky, they'd catch the sonofabitch by the end of the day. Or at least know who it was.

Shelby tucked her long hair behind her ear and turned to look behind them. When she swiveled back, Dev felt her gaze even with sunglasses shading her eyes.

"Are you worried we're being followed?" she asked.

"Just taking every precaution."

"Like last night when you drove in circles before going to your house."

"Yep." Though he hadn't driven in actual circles.

"*Are* we being followed?"

"Not that I can tell."

She faced fully forward once more, her hands clasped tightly in her lap while she stared out at the sunlit road. He could tell being in the apartment, seeing the threat on her mirror again, and talking to the cops had heightened her apprehension.

"You mentioned the veteran foundation earlier," he said as a distraction. "What do you do there?"

"A weekly vet check for the service dogs Grayson trains."

"That's cool. There's definitely a need for that."

"It's a great program. They've been able to place almost a dozen dogs so far, and have a few more almost ready for graduation."

"How long does it take to train them?"

"Depending on the dog, anywhere from eight to eighteen months."

"What are you checking every week when you visit?"

"Well, the dogs don't really need to be checked that often," she admitted, "But, it's a good excuse to spend time getting to know my brother, *and* I get to play with the puppies every week. My favorites are the German Shepherds. Grayson's Remy is amazing."

The animation in her voice had him shooting her a glance across the cab. "How come you don't have one of your own?"

"I wish, but between school, starting construction on my clinic, and then the animal hospital, I haven't had the time. It wouldn't be fair to the dog."

Understandable. "What's the deal with the clinic? I

94

remember my mom saying something about it, but that was last year already."

Shelby made a disgruntled sound. "It's been a bit of a mess. Permit delays, rezoning problems, and then I had to shut down construction when someone trashed the place just before Maverick was born almost two months early. Mae took a couple months off."

He shot her another look, his fingers tightening on the wheel. "Is that what your dad was talking about a couple weeks ago?"

"It was last October, but yeah. Someone went in with a sledgehammer and destroyed everything. Besides the structural foundation, we pretty much have to start over inside."

"They ever catch who did it?"

She shook her head. "After all the other issues, I decided to hold off for a bit and took the job at the vet hospital. But, Mae's crew is restarting construction next week, so it's definitely happening."

He kept her talking about the plans for the rest of the drive, though in the back of his mind he added the sabotage to a growing list of things to look into. The driveway to the Diamond estate was full of vehicles when they pulled in shortly before eleven a.m.

Dev walked with Shelby up to the door, but she caught his forearm when he reached for the handle. With the temps in the low fifties, he'd pushed up his sleeves, and the warmth of her touch on bare skin shot straight up his arm. He'd been mentally drilling himself not to touch her, and his first instinct was to jerk away. Recalling her earlier frown, he checked the action. The tight line of her mouth as she lowered her hand told him she still noticed his flinch.

"Please don't say anything about my apartment, okay?" she asked as she pushed her sunglasses up on top her head. "I don't want everyone freaking out instead of enjoying the after-wedding stuff."

"I'm actually going to go hang out with Reyes at the barn."

"Oh." She glanced toward the stables with a slight frown. "I thought he was sick. Was it just a twenty-four-hour bug then?"

Supposedly. Dev suspected he'd skipped Loyal's wedding for other reasons, but only shrugged in response to Shelby's question and pulled out his phone. "Gimmie your cell number."

As soon as she gave him the number, he sent her a text. "Now you got my number. Just text me when you're ready to leave."

She'd pulled out her phone to glance at the screen, then stuffed it back in her pocket. "Yeah, okay." For a second she sounded disappointed. But then she straightened her shoulders and lifted her chin to meet his gaze as she grasped the door handle. "That's perfect actually. Tell Rey I said hi. Glad he's feeling better."

He narrowed his gaze at the hint of mutiny in her expression. When she stepped inside, he warned, "I'm serious about the text, Shelby. Don't go anywhere alone."

Catching the door before it closed, she rolled her eyes. "I'm in the safest place I can be, Dev."

"Humor me. I'll meet you up *here* when you're ready, got it?"

She gave him a tight smile and a mocking salute, and then shut the door in his face.

Dev drew in a deep breath and let it back out again as he hung his head. Barely twelve hours into the job and she was driving him crazy. How the hell was he going to handle the next few days, or possibly even weeks?

The only way you can—help catch this guy sooner than later.

He lifted his head with determination and did a quick about-face to return to his truck. Before driving down to see his brother, he dialed the number Shelby's father had texted him shortly after he and Janine had left for the airport last night.

Rolling down the window, he braced his elbow on the door frame while it rang. Once the senator answered, he took a few minutes to brief him on what had happened the night before, and their time with the authorities earlier.

"How's she holding up?" Mark asked, concern in his voice.

"She's a little shook up, but doing okay."

"I'm grateful you're the one looking out for her. We've got a couple of major bills coming to the floor this week, otherwise I'd be back home with her under my roof in a heartbeat." It was obvious from his tone, he hated not being able to be there for his daughter. "Then again, she'd probably fight me tooth and nail on moving back home."

"I'll do whatever it takes to keep her safe," Dev assured him.

"It has to be twenty-four seven," Mark stated. "She's not going to like it, but no more picking her up and dropping her off like Blake and the others were doing. I want someone with her at all times. Preferably you."

"That's the plan. I have an Army buddy of mine installing a top of the line security system at my place right now. If she doesn't want to stay there, I'll do the same at her apartment."

"Good. Spare no expense and send me the bill when it's done."

"I'm not worried about that, Sir." Though he was a tad surprised the senator didn't bat an eye over them basically living together.

"Still, I'll cover whatever you deem necessary."

Dev murmured his agreement as he squinted toward the barn. Reyes walked through the open doors, leading one of the thoroughbreds out to pasture, past a car he now recognized as Solana's rental. "On a side note, do you recall a campaign staffer by the name of Chad Mayer?"

Papers rustled in the background as he replied, "Sure. He worked on the campaign from the start."

"You ever have any issues with him?"

"Not that I'm aware of. He's a nice kid. Did a great job getting people out to vote. Why?"

A sudden ache in his thigh had Dev absently rubbing his leg. "I'd like to have your PI check him out."

"What prompted this?"

"Just a vibe I got when I saw him talking to Shelby at the wedding last night."

"He was at the wedding?" The senator's voice held an obvious frown. "I don't recall his name on the guest list."

"Shelby said the same thing. He told her he was getting drinks with some friends."

"At The Piñon?"

Dev gave a wry grunt, watching his brother return to the stable. "That's what I said."

"Tell you what—I'll send you Gus' contact info and let him know you'll be in touch. Anything you need or want checked out, just let one of us know."

"Thanks. I'll keep you updated."

As soon as they hung up, he started the engine and drove to the barn. When he limped inside, he found Reyes in the office with his sister and dad—and his brother appeared remarkably well recovered.

His dad cradled a cup of coffee in his hands as he reclined back in the leather chair behind the desk. Lana rested one booted foot over the opposite knee, her fingers linked over her stomach in a relaxed pose. She grinned up at him when he squeezed her shoulder, her dark ponytail swishing across the vest she'd layered over a long-sleeved black shirt.

"What are you doing here today?" he asked his dad as he took a seat in the empty chair next to his sister.

"Your mom is up at the main house for the gift opening, so I was going to work on some paperwork until these two distracted me."

He shot Lana a questioning glance. "No gift opening for you? I figured for sure you'd be up visiting with Ceels and the guys." She'd been as close with Loyal and Asher as she'd been with Celia.

"I had my fill of wedding crap yesterday," she said with an airy wave of her hand. "I'd much rather chill with you guys before heading back tomorrow."

Washington State was her home base with the FBI, but she'd told them all yesterday she was on the short list for a transfer to the Denver field office. If that happened, it would be the first time they were all living back in Colorado since he'd joined the military twelve years ago. He had to admit, it would be nice to see Lana more than once or twice a year.

Reyes grabbed the coffee pot off the burner to pour himself a cup. "The real question is, bro, what are *you* doing here?"

"I brought Shelby over." At his dad's raised eyebrows, Dev added, "She stayed at my place last night."

That raised his brother's eyebrows.

"You and Bells, hey?" Lana said with a sly grin.

"Not like *that*," he growled. "I drove her home after the wedding when her bodyguard fucking flaked out. Good thing, too, because someone had broken into her apartment, so I took her to my house."

His sister's blue eyes sobered. "Damn. Is she okay?"

"Yeah. The cops are checking surveillance tapes for a suspect."

His dad sat forward, expression grim as he braced his elbows on the desk. "That's a scary situation all the way around."

"Yeah. This guy can't be caught soon enough." He motioned toward Reyes' cup. "Hook me up, man."

Reyes gave a disgruntled huff, but handed it over readily and poured himself another. "Sounds to me like you took the job."

"Yeah." Dev slouched back in his chair with a heavy sigh.

Lana glanced back and forth between them. "What job?"

Rey turned and leaned back against the small kitchenette counter. "Bells' bodyguard."

His dad's eyebrows soared upward once again. "When did this happen?"

"Mark asked me a few weeks ago, but I said no."

"Why? And what changed your mind?"

"He didn't think he could protect her," Reyes butt in before Dev could even open his mouth. As he glared at his brother, the shit answered the second question. "As for what changed his mind, I'm guessing all it took was one look at baby Bells all grown up in her bridesmaid's dress."

If he told him to shut the fuck up, he'd only be confirming what Reyes said. "Shelby has been grown up for years, you jackass."

Reyes grinned and raised his mug for a sip. A glance at Lana caught her smirk, too. Geezus. There was only five years between him and Shelby, so even if what they were inferring were true, it wasn't like he was some dirty old man robbing the cradle.

Their dad was still patiently waiting for his answer.

Dev grimaced. "I *wasn't* sure I could do the job," he admitted. "But last night proves I can do a hell of a lot better than the guy she had."

Dad shook his head. "There's no half-assing something like this, Dev."

The warning put him on the defensive. "I know that. I would never do anything to jeopardize your relationship with the Diamonds."

That prompted an impatient frown. "I'm not worried about that. But you know damn well, when the bar is set low, *a hell of a lot better* isn't how you measure your ability to do the job right."

His pulse skipped as he recognized the truth of those

words. Simply being better than Blake wasn't good enough.

His dad looked him square in the eye. "I have every confidence in your ability to keep Shelby safe, but that doesn't mean shit if *you* don't."

CHAPTER 12

*S*helby sat on one of the bar stools in the room her parents used for political entertaining, picking at a piece of leftover wedding cake as Loyal and Roxanna finished opening gifts. As always, Honor had worked her magic with the sweet treat, but guilt over being snotty to Dev when he dropped her off had killed her appetite.

He'd only been looking out for her safety, and she'd reacted badly to his order not to go anywhere alone because she'd been disappointed he wasn't coming inside with her. Truth was, she should've been relieved to avoid the questions her family would've asked when they walked in together. Especially after the brunch scene from three weeks ago, and the attention he'd paid her last night.

Besides, Dev was right. She couldn't let her guard down no matter where she was. She'd relaxed over the past couple of weeks knowing someone else was watching over her, but she needed to be more vigilant. Like last night, when he'd insisted on checking her apartment instead of just leaving her at the front door.

It struck her in that moment if he hadn't done that, she'd have been by herself when she found the message on her mirror. A chill snaked down her spine at the thought of having to face that alone.

Celia slid onto the empty stool on her right, snapping the ugly, frightening thread of Shelby's thoughts.

"Hey, sis. You're awfully quiet today."

"Just tired." And thankfully, she, Honor, and Mae had picked up her slack in the post-wedding bridesmaid duties. "I didn't get to bed until after two, and was back up again a little after seven. You and Robert were smart cutting out early."

Her sister leaned in closer, letting her dark, chin-length bob slide forward like a privacy curtain. "I was ovulating, so it was either leave early or have him take me in the back corner of the coat room."

Shelby winced and pushed her cake aside. "TMI, Ceels. TMI."

"Oh, stop acting like a virgin."

Raine joined them in time to overhear Celia's teasing reprimand. "She's not acting—unless Dev took care of that last night?"

Shelby tilted her head at their cousin in disbelief.

"Devante?" Her sister trained her brown gaze on Shelby, propped her chin in her hand, and wiggled her eyebrows. "Do tell."

"Would you two keep your voices down?" she grumbled. "There's nothing to tell."

"No?" Raine asked. "Then how come I saw you two pull up in his truck earlier?"

"Because Dad hired him as my bodyguard last night after Noelle stole my other bodyguard for a quickie on the job."

"Lucky you," her cousin quipped.

Shelby slid off the stool. "Yeah, lucky me. The stalker who sabotaged my car broke into my apartment and left a creepy message on my mirror, and my new, hot bodyguard flinches with revulsion every time he gets near me. Life's never been better." Self-pity choked out the last words.

Mortified at everything that had just spilled out of her mouth, she brushed past the two of them. Perfect. She'd told Dev not to say anything, and then *she* went and word vomited all over the place.

Without a thought beyond escape, she ended up in the kitchen. Celia and Raine followed fast on her heels.

"Shelby, wait." Her sister caught her arm and pulled her around to face them. "When did your apartment get broken into?"

She leaned her head back, blinking rapidly to stem the tears. Once she had her emotions under control, she did her best to gloss over the events of the past eight hours. "Last night. But I stayed at Dev's, and he called the police first thing this morning. It's being taken care of."

"I'm sorry," Raine said softly. "I didn't know things were *that* bad."

"Well, she doesn't have a bodyguard for the fun of it," Celia retorted.

"It's fine. *I'm* fine." She sniffed away the last of the tears. "And don't go saying anything to anyone. I don't want to make a big deal of this and disrupt things for Loyal and Rox."

"They'd be the first ones to say your safety is more important than wedding gifts," her sister argued.

"I know, but I am safe. Dad's got Dev on the job now."

Sarcasm rang in her voice. It wasn't fair, and she didn't even mean it the way it came out. She knew she was safer with him than Blake. Clearly, she was taking it personally every time he flinched away from her.

But how could she not?

He acted like she had a contagious disease.

She pushed that aside and spent the next few minutes assuring her sister and cousin everything was under control. Once she managed to convince them she just needed a moment alone to gather her composure, she pulled out her phone and texted Dev: *Ready.*

His reply came back within thirty seconds: *Be there in 5*

A small flutter in the pit of her stomach accompanied a rush of relief as she sent back: *I'm in the kitchen, so drive around to the back service entrance.*

She wasn't even going back out to the party to say goodbye. Knowing Celia, their brothers would get the low-down before the last gift was unwrapped, and she wanted to be long gone by then. Although their questions and advice came from a place of love, it was starting to get a little repetitive the third or fourth time around.

A loud creak from behind had her nearly jumping out of her skin. She whirled around with a gasp, phone clutched in her fist.

"*Perdōna, mija.*" Elena extended her hand, palm out. "I didn't mean to scare you."

Shelby sagged against the island counter at the sight of Dev's mom, her knees weak from the surge of adrenaline. Two seconds later, she found herself wrapped in the petite Spanish woman's arms. She clung to her, the comfort of her reassuring hug triggering a rush of unexpected emotion. With her own mom back in D.C., Elena was the next best thing.

"I didn't mean to eavesdrop, but I was in the pantry—"

Shelby pulled back with a low groan. "Please don't ask me if I'm okay."

Elena gave her a gentle smile. "I already know you're fine. I heard you say it at least three times. Possibly four."

"Well, I am." She looked away, and then recalled the rest of her conversation with Celia and Raine. *Crap.* "What I said about Dev…"

His mother arched a perfectly sculpted eyebrow while moving around to the other side of the island to grab a chocolate chunk cookie from a loaded tray. "What did you say about Dev?"

"I didn't mean to sound ungrateful. And I know he'll do a good job. It's just, well…" She shrugged her shoulders. "He can be a little, um…"

"Bossy? Overbearing? Arrogant?"

Shelby's lips quirked as she raised her gaze to meet Elena's across the counter. "Yeah."

"He always has been," she agreed. "I imagine it served him well in the Army, but it'll take him a while to realize this isn't the military."

"Oh, he knows. I'm not so sure he cares."

Elena's soft laugh faded to a sigh. "Unfortunately, it wasn't his choice to leave, so the transition may take a little longer."

A seed of sympathy took root with the reminder. She accused him of treating her like a five year old, but maybe next time she could stop herself from acting like one.

"You know, I recall you two palling around quite a bit when you were younger."

The thoughtful note in the older woman's musing brought forth her own memories—and a slight frown. "He was nice enough to tolerate me tagging after him. And that ended the moment he got his first girlfriend. He discovered cars and girls, and I was still playing with frogs."

His mother made a sound that was neither disagreement nor agreement. But she didn't know that things had really changed about the time Shelby hit thirteen, right after he'd graduated high school and left for the Army. And then there was the whole mortifying rejection at sixteen.

Elena braced her elbows on the counter while breaking off a small chunk of the cookie in her hand. But she didn't eat it as she raised her gaze. "Can I ask you to do something for me?"

The solemnity in her expression quickened Shelby's pulse. "Of course."

"Both my boys lost a part of themselves out there in the world."

It was strange to hear her call them *boys* when both Dev and Reyes were strong, capable men. And yet, to their mother, she guessed that's what they'd always be —her boys.

"I'm sure they've dealt with things you and I can't even imagine," Shelby murmured.

"I know that. And I worry it's too much for them to carry alone, but neither of them will open up to me or Estefan. They keep everything to themselves because they don't want us to worry."

"And that makes you worry more."

Elena nodded. She broke off another piece of cookie, then dropped all of it on the counter and brushed off her fingers as if realizing the mess she was making. "You'll be spending a lot of time with Dev now. Don't let him keep you at arm's length, okay? Maybe he'll open up to you."

"Things between us aren't anywhere near where he'd confide in me," Shelby advised. "I've asked him twice about his injury, and he refuses to tell me about it."

Elena's mouth tightened as her brow furrowed.

"Do you know what happened?" If Dev wouldn't tell her, maybe his mom would.

But she shook her head. "Not much of it, and even if I did, that's his to tell. I do know he's recovered physically beyond what the doctors expected."

That didn't surprise her one bit. Dev wasn't the kind of man who would react well to limitations. She didn't think there was much of anything that would keep him down.

"You were friends once," Elena said, her words almost a plea. "You can be friends again."

She wasn't so sure about that.

The sound of the back kitchen door opening had them both standing straighter as Dev entered. He gave Shelby a sweeping assessment before going over to give his mom a hug and a kiss on the cheek. A few words in Spanish had her smiling. Shelby wondered what he'd said as he reached to snitch a couple of cookies from the tray.

"I didn't make those for you," his mother admonished.

"But you always make extra for me and Rey," he argued as he bit into the first one.

"There are other guests this weekend."

"And you still made extra, didn't you?"

Shelby listened to their exchange with a smile that widened when Elena couldn't refute his claim about the cookies. His mother rolled her eyes, pulled a zipper bag from a nearby drawer, and proceeded to fill it with at least a dozen of the treats while he ate the two he'd stole.

When Dev reached for the bag, his mother blocked him and walked around the island to give it to Shelby.

"That's not fair," he protested.

Elena gave her another quick hug and whispered, "Make him earn them," before stepping back with a smile.

Shelby knew how she meant it, yet warmth climbed her neck as she considered alternative ways to make Dev earn the cookies. Shooting him a quick glance, her pulse skipped and tripped when she saw him watching her.

He slid his gaze to his mom, then back to her, and in a blink, he was all brusque business. "You said you were ready, so let's go."

"Dev," his mom admonished.

"What? She's the one who wanted to leave."

"I do. Thanks, Elena." She held up the bag as she started toward the door. "Especially for these. I'm going to enjoy every single one." She gave Dev a smirk with that last bit, but he was mid-reach to snatch a third cookie off the tray.

His mom slapped at his hand. "*Ladrón!*"

Cookie firmly in his grasp, he wore a grin of triumph when he caught up with Shelby at the door and reached around her to push it open. Her breath caught at the sight of that elusive smile up close, but then her shoulder brushed his chest, and the smile vanished as he stiffened.

His recoil dropped a heavy weight smack dab in the

middle of her chest, making her heart ache on their way outside. He opened the door of his truck for her, but there was no gentlemanly hand of assistance to climb on up.

"Let me hold those for you while you get in."

She angled her body to protect the bag of cookies from his grasp and gave him a mock glare. "Hands off, buddy."

He stepped back with an exaggerated sigh. "It was worth a try."

Shelby's automatic grin sobered with confusion while she secured her seatbelt and Dev made his way around to the driver's side. The contrast of his constant physical retreat against flashes of teasing was bewildering, and more than a little frustrating. Those tiny glimpses of how he used to be with her years ago made her long for more.

"Don't let him keep you at arm's length."

Elena's request was somewhat ironic she was coming to realize. Because of what had happened between her and Dev nine years ago, she was always quick to go on the defensive. Sometimes even the offensive. Better to have her guard up than risk getting hurt again.

But maybe if she relaxed a little, he would, too. In the personal sense, not the bodyguard sense.

It's worth a try.

"What does ladron mean?" she asked as he started the engine.

"*Ladrón,*" he corrected, a sexy Spanish accent stirring a flutter in the pit of her stomach. "It means thief."

"Well, your mom gave these to me, so don't get any ideas." She shifted the zipped baggie to the far right side of her lap as he drove down the driveway.

"That's a *lot* of cookies to eat all by yourself."

His tone had her arching her brows in offense. "What exactly are you saying?"

The corners of his mouth tugged upward. "I said exactly what I said."

And everything else between the lines. "I run a couple times a week, you know."

He shot her a stern frown. "Not for the foreseeable future you don't."

With those few clipped words, he ruined the mood. She didn't bother pointing out she could go to a gym as she turned to brood out the passenger window.

"On that note, you have some decisions to make."

A sarcastic snort came out louder than she intended, but she didn't care. "Really? *I* get to make a decision? You're not just going to *tell* me what's going on?"

"Yes, smartass, you get to make a decision."

"Ooh, goody." Shelby twisted toward him and rubbed her hands together. "About what? Which way you're turning up here? What we're having for dinner? What color scrubs I'm going to wear to work tomorrow?"

He flipped the blinker on for a left turn. "For starters, do you want to move in with me, or would you rather I move in with you?"

CHAPTER 13

Shelby blinked in genuine shock, her jaw slack as Dev made the turn and accelerated onto the highway. "*What?*"

"I talked to your dad," he explained as if they were discussing the weather. "Until this over, he wants someone with you at all times, and I agree with him. So... since you're stuck with me twenty-four seven, where do you want to live?"

Live with Dev. Twenty-four hours a day. Seven days a week.

Eating meals with him. Sleeping with him. Well...not sleeping *with* him.

Then again—

"Shelby?"

She blinked away the image of his bedroom only to have hers fill her vision. Front and center were the words scrawled in red across her vanity mirror. She knew they'd been wiped away after the cops left, but the image would be burned into her head forever.

"With you. I'll move in with you."

He gave a curt nod. "Okay. You want to go by your place for some of your things, or should I arrange for someone to bring them to my place?"

Dealing with a bodyguard whenever she'd wanted to leave her apartment had been frustrating and inconvenient. Now he would be shadowing every second of her life. Talk about feeling caged. She hadn't driven herself anywhere since the day Dev had pulled her SUV out of the ditch.

Since the day someone cut your power steering line.

She fisted her hands as she clenched her jaw against the urge to scream her resentment. More so at the situation than him, but all bets were off the next time he acted like she had leprosy.

"I can get my own stuff," she bit out. "And I guess I'll need my bed." Then again, she wasn't so sure she even wanted to sleep on that bed anymore. The idea of it creeped her out. Which pissed her off. "Actually, no, I'll buy a new one—if you don't mind stopping somewhere?"

"I already ordered a bedroom set for my guest room. It's being delivered tomorrow."

That was nice. Considerate. And yet, she tilted her head toward him, gaze narrowed. "You were that sure I'd"—she made air quotes—"*choose* your place?"

"I figured I could use a guest bed no matter what."

"Sure. Okay."

He didn't bother to argue against the sarcasm in her voice, which only confirmed her suspicion. The thought of him patronizing her with bogus 'choices' triggered another spike of annoyance. She'd rather he go back to issuing orders.

Maybe.

When they reached her apartment, she attempted to use that irritation to battle rising nerves, but then couldn't quite force her feet over the threshold.

Dev's hand settled at the small of her back. Her pulse skipped, but she had no time to marvel at the comforting gesture before steady, firm pressure guided her inside. He waited at her bedroom door as she moved toward the closet.

"Pack for a couple of weeks," he advised. "Just in case."

After dragging out her large suitcase, she started with scrubs for work, jeans and leggings, then moved on to T-shirts and sweatshirts. And, *just in case*, she added two dresses and the pair of four-inch, black Louboutin stilettos her parents had given her for Christmas.

She'd moved over to her dresser for underwear when her phone buzzed in her pocket. A quick glance revealed a text from her cousin.

Raine: *You left without saying goodbye.*

Shelby: *Sorry. I assume Celia spread the word, and I didn't want to deal with everyone's concern.*

Raine: *She's actually telling your brothers right now. I'm guessing you're still going to hear from them.*

She sighed and leaned a hip against her dresser as she replied: *Probably. Anyway, thanks and love you. Have a safe flight back to TX.*

Raine: *Thanks, and love you, too. But before I sign off...I can't stop thinking about what you said earlier.*

Shelby: *Honestly, Raine, I'm fine*—delete, delete, delete, delete—*good.*

Raine: *This isn't about your psycho stalker. It's about your hot new bodyguard.*

115

Of *course* she would eventually come around to that part of her earlier pity party. Shelby stared at the words on her screen. Though Dev was leaning against the door frame and nowhere close enough to see them, heat spread through her body as she snuck a glance his way from under her lashes.

With his eagle eye, that's all it took to put him on instant alert. He straightened and started toward her. "What is it?"

"Nothing," she exclaimed a little louder than necessary. She jerked up a hand to stay his approach. "It's just Raine texting."

He stopped, his narrowed gaze flicking down to her phone.

Slightly panicked he might insist on seeing the texts, she blustered, "You don't have to stand right here like my jailor, you know. You can wait in the living room."

It felt like a lifetime before he finally pivoted and left the room.

Relief flowed through her veins. She blew out a breath and turned her attention back to the screen to tap out a quick reply: *Strike that from your memory. I never said that.*

Her phone buzzed again, only this time her cousin's image popped up on the screen for an incoming call.

Shelby hurried to close the bedroom door as she answered with a furious whisper. "I'm not discussing this."

"But I have this theory," Raine insisted. "And Celia agrees with me."

"You two need to mind your own business." She crossed back to her dresser and scooped up a handful of underwear and bras to stuff in her suitcase.

"I think he doesn't trust himself to get too close. Especially if you consider why the other bodyguard got the boot."

Shelby frowned on her way back for socks. "That's ridiculous."

"No it's not. The man couldn't take his eyes off you last night."

"He was watching me because he had to."

"Not like *that* he didn't have to."

Her pulse skipped as she dropped the socks on top her underwear. "Like what?"

"Like he couldn't wait to get you alone."

She rolled her eyes and shook her head. "Too bad your theory doesn't test out. He had me alone last night and acted like I had leprosy."

"Because in his mind, it's a line he can't cross no matter how bad he might want to. I'm telling you, I'm spot on."

"And I'm guessing you've been drinking."

"Only one glass of champagne—I swear."

She snorted her disbelief.

"I'm serious, Bells. Put on something sexy, and you'll have him eating from the palm of your hand in no time."

Yeah, because that had worked so well the first time around. "I'm hanging up now."

"Love you. Good luck."

She disconnected and shoved her phone in her back pocket. A quick reach closed the suitcase lid, and she zipped it shut with jerky movements. Mid-lift off the bed, she paused and eyed her dresser. In the very back of her underwear drawer was the nude-colored satin nightie she'd worn back when she was sixteen. The first and only piece of sexy lingerie she'd ever bought. She should've tossed it, or burned it, or something, but had never quite been able to bring herself to get rid of it.

And now it was there. Something sexy. Just waiting to be worn again.

Would it even still fit?

Leaving the suitcase on the bed, she crossed the floor and reached for the drawer as her phone buzzed. Because it was easier to check the message than follow through with what she was considering, she pulled out her phone to see Raine's new text: *Seduce that man!*

"Almost done?"

Dev's voice from the doorway made her jump. A quick grab saved her phone from tumbling to the floor, and she quickly shoved it in her pocket, her heart racing like mad.

"Almost. I just want to grab a few more things."

Feeling a bit like a pinball, she went back to the closet to pull out a second suitcase for bathroom items and other personal mementos while he took her first suitcase out to the living room. Alone again, she snatched the lingerie from her drawer to tuck in the bottom of her suitcase, under the well-worn afghan Grandma Irene had given her for her sixteenth birthday.

They each carried a case out to his truck, and a half-hour later they were back at his house.

A black SUV sat in his driveway, and as Dev parked, she read Brennan Security Services lettered on the door. She didn't ask, and he didn't explain as he grabbed both suitcases to bring inside. Shelby had a strong suspicion her father was somehow involved in whatever this development involved. Something state of the art, no doubt. The best money could buy.

It was nothing to be upset about, but how was it that

this was already in motion when she'd made the decision to stay at Dev's less than an hour ago?

"Brennan?" Dev called out as they walked inside and he shut the door.

"Over here."

The voice came from near the French doors that led from the kitchen nook to the backyard. A dark-haired man with a close-cropped beard glanced over his shoulder at the two of them. "Hey, Torrez. I'm nearly done."

"Make yourself at home," Dev said to Shelby as he set her suitcases down. "I'll take care of this while you get settled."

He crossed the floor to the kitchen, and when the other guy rose, they clasped hands like they were going to arm wrestle. Instead they pulled in to give each other firm thumps on the back. Shelby snuck glances of their exchange as she hung up her coat before ambling to the kitchen island to set down the baggie of chocolate chunk cookies.

Brennan stepped back, his gaze flicking to Dev's legs as his brows shot up. "Wow. Look at you after only three fucking months." He shot a glance toward Shelby. "Shit. Language. Sorry."

She smiled and shrugged.

Dev rotated slightly toward her. "Jensen Brennan, Shelby Diamond. We served together for six years."

Totally explained the camaraderie. Shelby moved forward, meeting him halfway for a polite handshake. "Nice to meet you," she murmured.

"Likewise." Jensen turned back to Dev, hands propped on his hips. "You are fucking Superman."

Dev shifted his stance, clearly uncomfortable. "The doctors underestimated, that's all. You said you're almost done?"

The pointed change of subject had Jensen giving Shelby another quick look before turning back to the French doors. "Yeah. Give me five minutes, and then I'll show you what this bad boy can do."

His words overshadowed her curiosity over Dev's apparently miraculous recovery. They were clear evidence that what had been presented to her earlier as a choice was quickly proving to be nothing more than a placating pat on the head.

Jensen disappeared into one of the bedrooms, and Shelby planted herself in front of Dev, arms crossed over her chest. "Did you figure you could use a souped-up security system no matter what, too?"

His brow furrowed until she saw understanding dawn in his eyes. "Does it matter?"

"Apparently not. I just want you to admit you weren't *actually* going to give me a choice."

"Of course the choice was yours. Still is."

"Um hm."

His jaw tightened as he tilted his head, "Do you want to go back to your place?"

"I didn't say that."

"Do you want to rent a whole new apartment? Or move back home?" He threw his hands up from his sides and stalked over to pick up her suitcases. "Tell me what you want, Shelby, and that's what we'll do."

"The place is not the issue," she exclaimed as he stood there with her bags hanging from his grip. "I hate being patronized, that's all."

"I wasn't patronizing you," he insisted. "I swear to God, if you had wanted to stay at your place, I would've had security installed there, too. It was a fifty-fifty chance, and going off your reaction last night, I bet on my place first."

The words sank like a pit in her stomach. He'd correctly guessed her choice, not made it for her. She stood there feeling like an idiot for making a big deal out of what two seconds later seemed like nothing.

Dev dropped her stuff and closed some of the distance between them. "I know this isn't easy on you, but picking a fight with me isn't going to help."

She nodded as she grimaced at her bags. Reminded herself to act like a mature adult, not a child.

"Shelby."

Dev's gentle tone drew her gaze back to his.

"Listen, I get it. I know what it's like to not have a say in something so monumental it turns your life upside down."

His involuntary medical discharge from the Army. Her chest tightened at the genuine sympathy in his low voice, and *she* wanted to hug *him*.

"I can't help that you're going to be restricted until this is over," he continued, "but I'm not going to take anything away from you unless it impacts your safety. And, I promise I'll be straight with you on everything, but you gotta trust me, too."

Trust him. That was hard when she was thoroughly confused about so many things. She lifted her gaze to his, her pulse speeding up as a question formed in her head. *The* question. A swipe of her tongue wet her dry lips in preparation to ask, but then his attention dropped to her mouth, and suddenly he'd taken another step closer.

The air seemed too heavy to draw into her lungs, and her heart banged hard against her ribs when his gaze locked on her mouth as he leaned in.

"All right, everything is rea-dy." Jensen stopped abruptly, halfway across the room. "Sorry. Didn't mean to interrupt."

Dev blinked and jerked back with a muttered, "You didn't." His shuttered gaze met hers for a split-second before he turned to his friend. "Walk me through the system so you can get out of here and enjoy what's left of your Sunday."

CHAPTER 14

Monday evening, Dev slid sideways when Shelby joined him at the kitchen sink while he washed the pan she'd used to make their grilled cheese and ham sandwiches for dinner. He angled his body to keep her small shoulder from brushing his, but she ate up the extra room by sliding closer as she reached to turn on the faucet to rinse their plates before loading them in the dishwasher.

He drew in a controlled breath and rested his wet hands against the far side of the sink while moving over even farther. Since she cooked, he was supposed to clean up, but here she was, ignoring him.

Just like she'd been ignoring him on other shit, too. Little shit. Which wouldn't be such a big deal, *if* she wasn't also pushing him every chance she got since yesterday afternoon. Ever since he'd nearly given in to the urge to kiss her. Thank God for his buddy's impeccable timing.

He'd told her to make herself at home, and man, she'd taken the invite to heart, in more ways than one. She was constantly getting too close for his comfort and invading his personal space—always with a valid reason that he couldn't quite challenge.

Although he'd managed to avoid physical contact for the most part, the addicting scent of her apple-peachy shampoo was chipping away at his sanity with each passing hour.

She'd taken a personal day from work today, which meant they'd spent a second entire day together. Breakfast, lunch, dinner. Getting everything set up in the guest bedroom, including putting together the new bed. With all the space in his twenty-five hundred square foot house, she had somehow managed to remain within ten feet of him most of the time.

Last night she'd spent the evening flipping through channels while he attempted to read. Turned out it was impossible to concentrate with her only a few feet away, so he'd gone into the gym for his evening session of physical therapy. She'd left him alone for that, but then he found himself right back in the same room as her when it was time for bed.

She still hadn't wanted to sleep alone, so he'd dragged out his sleeping bag and mat to lie on the floor next to the bed. Three minutes later, he'd returned from brushing his teeth to find her zipped up to her chin in his spot.

Her back turned to him was a clear indication she would argue about staying on the floor until she was blue in the face. It went against every fiber of his being, but he'd zipped his lips and climbed into bed. Her fucking choice, right? Let her have it.

Only, then it took him hours to fall asleep as he lay there feeling guilty.

This morning, he'd gotten up early so he could do his PT before driving her to work, only to have her join him in his home gym. She'd simply said, "I'm not going in to work today," and started stretching in a pair of black yoga pants and a neon pink, skin tight exercise crop top that zipped up the front. By the time she flipped the switch on his treadmill to start jogging, he was hard as a rock.

The thing was, he wasn't quite sure if she was doing it all deliberately, or if she was just being Shelby. Beautiful, innocently sexy, contradiction-filled Shelby.

He still wasn't sure nearly twelve hours later.

She bent to put the rinsed plates in the dishwasher rack, and he had to bite back a groan when he found his gaze drawn straight to the curve of her ass in a pair of black leggings. Leaving the pan in the sink, he scooped up a dry towel for his hands and moved to stand by the stove.

"I have a few things to take care of tomorrow while you're at work, so Reyes is going to be with you for a couple hours instead."

She closed the door and straightened, bracing one hip against the counter. "Does he really need to be there? I mean, I'll be surrounded by coworkers."

"And how many people you don't know coming and going with their pets."

"Okay, so he needs to be there." Her lips pressed together as she turned to the sink and started washing the pan he'd abandoned. "Where are you going?"

He hesitated before keeping his promise to be straight with her. "I'm meeting with your dad's PI, and I have a therapy session at one."

Her hands stilled, then scrubbed the clean pan harder. "Physical therapy?"

"No."

She reached to turn on the faucet to rinse the pan. "You talk to a therapist?"

"Once a week."

The surprise in her expression had him wishing he'd kept his damn mouth shut. There was being straight with her, and then there was stupidity. Now she was going to think he was all fucked up in the head. Time with his therapist had helped him realize he wasn't doing too bad, and things were getting better each week.

Tossing the towel on the counter, he moved past her to head into the living room.

"Do your parents know?" she asked.

He shrugged. "I don't know that they've ever asked."

The water shut off. "So you don't tell them unless they specifically ask?"

Disapproval rang in her tone, and his defenses rose as he paused with a backward glance. "It isn't something I broadcast. I'm dealing with things and getting on with my life."

She braced her hands on the counter, accusation in her eyes. "Do you have any idea how much your mother worries about you? You *and* Reyes."

He pivoted to face her fully as a memory flashed in his mind. "Is that what you two were talking about when I walked in on Sunday?" He got his answer when her gaze wavered and she took a sudden interest in wiping the counter. His gut tightened at the thought of them discussing his life behind his back. "I thought it was too quiet the second I walked through the door."

"You should let her know you're seeing someone," she said quietly.

"Why me?" he retorted. "I'm sure she'll be just as glad to hear it from you."

"It's not my place to tell her." She shot him a glance, but looked away again just as fast. "Like it wasn't her place to tell me what happened to you."

"You asked her?" Another surge of anger stalked him back to the island where he flattened his palms on the counter. "Why do you want to know so bad? What will it matter?"

The thought of her possibly seeing him as less than capable made his stomach ball in a knot. It was precisely why he'd shoved his cane in the back of his closet early Sunday morning and hadn't taken it out since.

Apprehension and curiosity shone in her brown eyes. "I don't know. Maybe I'll understand better."

"Understand what?"

She swallowed hard enough for him to hear it. "You're different. You've changed from when we were kids."

"I've been to war and back, Shelby. Thirty-seven times."

Her eyes widened, showing she really had no clue what his life had been like. Not many people did.

Because you've never told them.

He wasn't complaining. Hell, he'd still be doing it if he had the choice. But some—*much*—of what he'd seen and done wasn't something you shared with the people you love.

His mind rejected that last part, and he took it out on her. "You want to know so damn bad, then I'll tell you. But I don't want your fucking pity, you got it?"

She gave a jerky nod, her gaze trained on his face.

Well, fuck. Now there was no turning back.

He shifted sideways to drop down onto one of the barstools, then braced his elbows on the counter and scrubbed his hands over his face before resting them on the counter to glare at her. "My team specialized in hostage rescue. On my last mission, we were tasked with retrieving the wife and children of a high level terrorist. The wife was offering information in exchange for asylum for her and her three daughters."

Concern darkened her eyes. "Weren't you worried it could be a setup?"

"Always. But intel on the subject indicated she'd be a good asset, so we went in. The plan was in and out in seven minutes." He closed his eyes as the mission played in his head on super fast-forward—until it slowed. "Five minutes and forty-two seconds in, the oldest daughter got scared and broke free to run back. I followed and saw her father shoot her as she begged for forgiveness at his feet."

Shelby's gasp had him opening his eyes to see her cover her mouth in horror.

"I didn't give him a chance to beg," he stated through a throat full of gravel. He'd shot the bastard right between the eyes without an ounce of remorse. The truth of that rang in his voice, and one look at Shelby's face confirmed she understood the full meaning of his harsh words.

But he didn't allow himself time to assess her reaction. He was afraid she might not agree with what he'd done, and only see him as no better than the monster who'd killed his daughter.

"The guy got off a short burst before…"–*I put him down* —"he went down. I retrieved the daughter's body for her mother, and my team retrieved me. The surgeons in Germany reconstructed my knee and inserted a rod in my left femur, told me I'd be lucky if I walked again, and my career was over."

Outrage filled her eyes as her mouth gaped open. "They actually said that to you?"

"Not in those exact words, but that's what it boiled down to. I'd seen it happen to other guys, so I knew what was what." Not that it had helped cushion the blow. If anything, knowing had made it worse, because he knew the futility of fighting the inevitable.

"I'm so sorry, Dev."

And there it was. The softening of her eyes, the forward lean, the reach across the counter for his hand. He stared as her fingers slid closer. He craved the comfort of her touch so bad. Hell, he'd probably dream about it tonight, but it was a line he couldn't allow himself to cross. Once over, he'd never go back.

He jerked away, banging his elbow on the back of the chair in the process. "I told you I don't want your pity."

She straightened stiffly. "Offering sympathy is not the same as feeling sorry for someone. I don't feel sorry for you, but...it must've been awful to see that girl killed like that."

The direction of her empathy caught him off guard. "I've seen worse," he said gruffly.

Sorrow darkened her brown eyes. "I don't imagine that makes it any easier."

A lump formed in his throat as he shook his head in confirmation. He shoved to his feet and turned away before she could see the tears stinging his eyes.

Damn it. He didn't want her understanding. Or her sympathy. Or the possibility of her accepting who he was now only to later have the darkness inside him destroy her light.

"I'm going to do my PT."

Just before he reached the hall, she called his name. "Dev. Can I ask you something?"

The slight plea in her voice halted his steps. "I'd rather you not."

But then he stayed right there, unable to force his feet to move forward again.

A moment later, her slippered footsteps sounded behind him. He turned, and when she got within an arm's-length away, he took a step back. She drew to an abrupt halt, hurt flashing in her eyes before her lashes swept down to conceal them. That glimpse of vulnerability stabbed him straight in the heart.

"Yesterday, you promised you'd be straight with me," she reminded.

Yeah. Stupidest promise he'd ever made. "Ask what you're going to ask."

She swallowed hard, then took a breath as she looked up, as if she had to gather her courage to speak. "You pull away every time I get too close. Is it me specifically you don't want to touch, or did something happen that keeps you away from everyone?"

In for a penny, in for a pound, isn't that how the saying went?

Since he was fucked no matter what, he gave it to her exactly as he'd promised. "It's definitely you. Because if I let myself touch you even once, I'm not going to want to stop."

CHAPTER 15

"*If I let myself touch you, I'm not going to want to stop.*"

So why the hell was she now huddled in the guest bed all alone as the clock ticked toward midnight?

Because when Dev was finished with his PT, he acted like that entire conversation never even happened. He was polite but distant—physically *and* emotionally. It was as if what he'd shared with her drove him further away instead of drawing them closer.

Which left her no closer to understanding, and when he went to bed an hour ago, she was hesitant to admit she was still apprehensive about being alone. She had wanted so badly to follow him to his room, even if she had to sleep on the floor again. Instead, she forced herself to turn into the guest room with the brand new bedroom set he'd ordered just for her.

Time to be a big girl.

Except, if she wasn't thinking about Dev, her mind went straight to her stalker. With the light still on beside the bed, she eyed the bare window as she hugged her knees to her chest. Too bad there hadn't been curtains or a shade to go with the comforter set that had arrived with the bedroom furniture.

The murky black square gaped at her, a frightening glass hole in the wall even with the new security system. After another glance at the time on her phone screen, she decided enough was enough. Swiping up her grandma's afghan, she padded over to see if she could somehow cover the glass. Her heart pounded faster as she got closer, but it only took a moment to realize she'd never reach the top without a chair.

Tossing the afghan on the bed, she started toward the kitchen for one of Dev's bar stools. She'd left the bedroom door ajar and it swung open with a low, extended squeak. Other than that, the house was dark and quiet, save for the ticking clock she'd never actually located. When she caught sight of the drawn shades in the living room, she paused. It only took a second to decide to retrieve the afghan and a pillow for the couch. Much easier—and quieter—than dragging one of those heavy stools into the bedroom.

She pulled the door closed behind her and latched it with the softest of clicks. Over at the couch, she tossed the pillow down before lifting her arms to shake out the afghan and lie down.

"What are you doing?"

Shelby let out a shriek at the sound of Dev's voice behind her. Her heart jammed up into her throat as she whirled around to find him watching her. "You scared the crap out of me."

"What are you doing?" he repeated.

A shift of his stance drew her gaze down. He had his hands clasped behind his back, and he wore only a pair of red boxer briefs that fit like a second skin. Noticing the bulge in the front of those briefs made her cheeks burn, but then she spotted the scars from his injury and surgery. Belatedly, she recalled how much he resented her staring, and she jerked her gaze back up to his face.

"I, um…" She tightened her arms around the afghan clutched to her chest. "I'm going to sleep on the couch."

He frowned toward the guest room. "Is there something wrong with the bed?"

"No. The bed is fine. It's just…there are no curtains or shades." She gave a self-conscious shrug. "I know it's stupid, but it freaks me out that someone could be watching me."

"It's not stupid at all," he corrected. "I'm sorry I didn't think of it."

"Well, I didn't either, until I was in the room by myself."

"I can hang a blanket over the window for tonight," he offered.

She shook her head quickly and backed up to sit on the couch. "It's okay, this is fine. Sorry if I woke you."

"I wasn't sleeping yet."

"Oh." She sat for a moment, then busied herself arranging the pillow and blanket. Better that than drooling over his bare chest, gorgeous arms, and ripped abs. Or taking a longer look at his red briefs.

He stood there, contemplating her with one hand still behind his back. Flutters kicked up in her stomach just before he released a soft sigh.

"Is it just the window?"

She futzed with the blanket some more before admitting, "No." A little spurt of anger had her thumping her hands on her lap before clasping them together. "I hate this. I'm not usually such a wimp. I lived alone for the past few months. I was practically alone at my parents' house a year before that, when they were spending most of their time in Washington."

"I don't think you're a wimp."

"Well, I feel like one."

Tick.

Tick.

Tick.

Tick.

Finally, she glanced his way. When she met his gaze, Dev gave a sideways jerk of his head, toward the hall. "Come on."

She couldn't go back in there alone. No matter how much she wished she could. She twisted to readjust the pillow. "I'll be fine here on the couch."

"I'm not talking about the guest room, Shelby. We both need to get some sleep."

Her whole body flashed hot, but she only hesitated a moment before gathering her blanket and pillow to walk across the floor toward him. He made a sweeping gesture with his arm for her to go first, and she noticed once again that his other still remained behind his back.

She glanced over her shoulder when he fell in step behind her. "Do you have your gun?"

He lifted one of those nicely muscled shoulders. "What kind of bodyguard would I be if I heard a noise and came out here empty handed?"

"You don't have to hide it from me."

"I didn't want to scare you."

When she paused a few feet inside his bedroom, he brushed past and walked to the side of the bed closest to the window. He set the weapon within reach on his nightstand, no longer trying to hide it from her sight.

"Guns don't scare me. It's the person who holds the gun that can be scary." Realizing what she'd said, she quickly added, "But not you—you don't scare me."

"No?" He arched his eyebrows, the tiniest bit of humor playing about his mouth. "Then why are you standing way over there?"

Because for as many times as she'd fantasized about being in the same bed with him, she'd never imagined it would actually happen. The flutters in her stomach were making her nauseous. She thought about asking for his sleeping bag and mat again, but come on, she was an adult. She could handle sleeping in the same bed as the guy she'd been half in love with since she first discovered makeup and boys 'round about age twelve.

Plus—the floor had sucked last night.

She crossed to the bed without another word. Realizing she clutched her grandma's afghan like a blankie, she tossed it over the end of the bed and slid between the sheets as Dev got in on his side. He turned out the bedside lamp, then settled down beside her.

Shelby's pulse thundered so loud in her ears, she was positive he heard it, too. She shifted carefully, afraid to brush up against him.

And then she almost laughed. Here she'd spent the whole day doing her best to get up in his space on purpose, and now she was nervous to move one inch in case her foot brushed against his under the covers.

She lay there, heart pounding, mind whirling, wondering how in the hell was she going to fall asleep?

"What's the matter?" Dev's voice rumbled in the dark.

"Nothing."

"You're stiff as a board. And you can breathe, Shelby. Relax. Go to sleep."

Breathe. Good idea.

She concentrated on drawing in a breath and letting it back out. Only she blew it out too fast and needed another one. And her heart was still racing, and her fingers were tingling, and—*oh my God, why the hell am I crying?*

Next thing she knew, Dev pulled her into his arms, her head on his chest, and his voice in her ear.

"Take a deep breath," he urged. "Come on, you can do it."

She sucked oxygen in.

"Now hold it. One, two, three, four. Let it out."

Once she blew it out, he had her repeat the process.

"Feel my chest." He inhaled deep. "Do what I'm doing, hold it, count two, three, four. Let it out."

The soothing tone of his voice, coupled with the steady rise and fall if his chest, helped slow her racing heartbeat so she could think straight again.

"I'm sorry," she whispered, sneaking her hand up to wipe her damp cheeks before resting it on his chest below her chin. "I feel like I have no control over anything anymore."

He smoothed his hand over her hair, much like when he'd comforted her the night of Loyal's wedding. "It'll get better. I promise. This isn't going to last forever."

She nodded, and focused on the soothing rhythm of his heartbeat beneath her ear.

The warmth of his musky skin beneath her cheek.

The firm muscles beneath her palm.

It dawned on her she was half-draped over his almost naked body, and suddenly she was afraid to move again. Afraid he'd pull away and reject her all over again.

Breathe.

She wasn't sure if he spoke out loud, or she simply heard his voice in her head, but she took measured breaths, relaxed, and slowly, finally drifted off to sleep. Somewhere in between, she swore she felt the press of his lips just above her temple.

CHAPTER 16

$\mathcal{D}$ev met Reyes at the reception desk of the animal hospital fifteen minutes before he needed to leave the next day.

"Shelby's in surgery at the moment, so all you need to do is keep an eye on who's coming and going. And after that, just be there if she needs you."

"Bells in surgery," Reyes repeated as he followed him toward the back. "I know she's a vet, but that still sounds strange."

Dev one hundred percent understood. He'd gotten quite the eye-opening this morning himself—and not only because waking up with her warm body snuggled against him felt so fucking right.

Knowing she was a veterinarian wasn't quite the same as seeing her in action. That, more than anything, drove home the fact she wasn't a kid anymore. Of course, he'd recognized the obvious on one level, but he'd still been thinking of her as that naïve sixteen-year-old girl who had no clue what she was asking of him in her bedroom that day.

Watching her work had him seeing her in a whole new light. Clients, animals, and co-workers alike were treated with kindness and compassion. About a half-hour ago, a dog had been rushed in that had been attacked by another dog. She seized control with a calm confidence that had her collogues looking to her for guidance, even though she was probably younger than many of them.

It was then he realized he needed to figure out a way to give her back some control in her personal life, or her anxiety would only get worse. For her sake, he'd hate to see it take over this part of her life, too.

After they left the front waiting area, Dev showed his brother where he could keep watch while Shelby finished her surgery. Reyes nodded to a couple of vet techs who eyed them with open curiosity.

"Everyone here is cool with this?" he asked with a quick glance around.

"We had a meeting with her boss first thing this morning. He said the staff was informed of the situation, and other than being extra vigilant if someone was acting odd, everyone was advised to go about their business as usual. People are curious, but they've been respectful."

"All right, then. I'll hold down the fort until you get back."

"Thanks. I have a stop to make after my therapist appointment, but I'll be back before her shift ends at three."

Reyes averted his gaze at the mention of a therapist. And while Dev made a point to mention it whenever he could, he didn't push, because that had gotten him nowhere over the past couple years. All he could do was let his brother know he was seeing someone after his own trauma, and show no shame in it. Hopefully, Reyes would choose to get the help he needed soon.

As he left the parking lot, Dev glanced at the animal hospital in the rearview mirror. Even knowing Shelby was in good hands—Rey was one of the few he'd trust her safety to—he still didn't like leaving her when the cops hadn't been able to get anything useful from the surveillance at her apartment building.

Ironic how quickly he'd gone from refusing the job to going all in.

Whoever it was threatening her, they knew how to cover their tracks well. Which had him extra eager to talk to Mark's private investigator. He'd called him Sunday evening to look into Chad Mayer and expected to get some results in the upcoming meeting.

Gus Landrum had gone to high school with the senator way back when. He'd gone on to the police academy while Mark went to college for business before eventually getting into politics.

The muddy-haired PI was in his mid-fifties, nearly six feet tall, and looked fit enough to still wear the badge even though he'd retired as a detective nearly five years ago. He'd done some security work for Mark when he was governor, and then opened his own private investigation agency shortly after the election for Senate.

Unfortunately, Gus had no good news for him.

"You're absolutely sure Mayer checks out?" Dev leaned forward with a frown. "Because I got some seriously bad vibes from that guy."

Bad vibes, or were you jealous?

The PI flipped open a red folder in front of him and slid it across his desk. "None of the flower shops that delivered her flowers recognized him, and his phone records are clean—other than the time Shelby said they went to dinner last summer. Plus, he had an alibi for both the night her power steering was cut, and the night of the wedding. Hell—you saw him at the wedding."

"I didn't keep an eye on him for the whole night," Dev argued as he scanned the page in front of him that confirmed exactly what Gus had just relayed. "He could've left right after Shelby and I went back to the reception."

"His drink tab was closed out at twelve-thirty-four a.m."

Right about the time he and Shelby left—which would've given the guy no time to break into her apartment, leave his insidious message, and get out again before they arrived.

He flipped the folder closed, shot it back across the desk, and rose with a muttered, "Fuck."

"Listen man, something will pop—it always does. In the meantime, you just do your job, and I'll keep doing mine. We'll get the motherfucker."

Dev raked a hand through his hair and rubbed at the tension throbbing at the base of his skull. "Do you have any other leads? I don't care how insignificant they sound, is there anything you've come across that seems the least bit off?"

Gus dug under a couple of folders and pulled out a light blue one that was three times as thick as the red one. "I had just started to review these before you called about Mayer."

He moved closer to the desk, flipped the folder open,

then read the top page. It was a photo copy of a death threat that had been sent to the senator about six months after he took office. Dev scanned the words, then flipped to the next page to see the same type of letter. He fanned the remaining pages, guessing there to be a good sixty to seventy letters.

"Are these all threats against Mark specifically?" he asked.

"A few reference his family," Gus said, "so I was going to focus on them first. Top fifteen or so are actual physical threats that have been investigated and dealt with by the Capitol police in D.C. After that, they're a little less severe. Angry bordering on threatening. I figured it couldn't hurt to have a second look at all of them."

"Any chance I can get copies and read through them, too?"

"Be my guest. Copier is around the corner."

When Dev had a folder of his own filled with copies still warm from the machine, he returned the blue file to Gus.

"Let me know if anything stands out to you," the PI said.

"Definitely. And I'd appreciate any updates as they come available on your end."

"You got it. Anything that keeps Shelby safe."

Back in his truck, he set the folder on the passenger seat, then thought better of it and tucked it behind his seat before heading to his one-o'clock appointment with his therapist. When he admitted he'd taken the bodyguard job over the weekend, Bryan looked up from the tablet perched on his thigh.

"What prompted that change?"

"The guy guarding her was doing a shit job."

"And you figured you could do better?" Bryan asked.

"Shelby deserves better."

"That doesn't answer my question. Three weeks ago you didn't trust your physical capabilities enough to take the job. What's changed, other than the fact you don't have your cane with you?"

"I don't need the cane anymore," he said, as much for himself as for Bryan. "If I didn't step up to protect her and something happened, I'd never forgive myself."

Shrewd blue eyes narrowed. "You care for her?"

"Of course. Our families are close." Dev shrugged, but couldn't quite bring himself to look the guy in the eye. The last time they'd talked about this, it had been about the job, and his self-doubts, not about Shelby and what feelings he might have for her. "Even though she's five years younger than me, we still grew up together."

Bryan adjusted the tablet on his leg, typed a few notes, then sat back and lifted his gaze. "What if something happens and you're not able to protect her?"

"I will."

"It's not guaranteed."

He'd make sure it was. His therapist shifted his gaze down, and Dev realized he was absently rubbing his injured thigh. He stopped the movement and consciously fought to keep from fisting his fingers.

"Where is she now?" Bryan asked.

"At work."

"And you're here."

He sat forward with a frown, bracing his elbows on his knees. "I didn't leave her there alone. My brother is with her until I get back."

"You trust your brother? Reyes, right?"

"Yeah—and obviously I trust him, or I wouldn't have left her." Dev shifted to the edge of his seat, fighting the urge to get up and leave. "What the fuck, man? Why are you trying to make me doubt myself?"

"I can't make you do anything, so if you have doubt..."

He shook his head, his humorless laugh loaded with irritation. "I thought you'd be happy I made forward progress with this. Hell, *you* agreed with my brother that I should've taken the job right from the start."

"Yes. But you need to acknowledge that there is a possibility something may happen that you can't control."

"Special Forces, remember? Expect the unexpected."

Bryan smiled with a slight nod of acknowledgment.

"Nothing about this past week has been what I expected," he admitted as he looked out the window toward the mountains. "But I *have* considered the possibilities. Multiple ways, multiple times."

"And?"

"Same conclusion no matter what—I'll do whatever it takes to keep her safe."

"*Can* you do what it'll take to keep her safe?"

Dev turned his gaze back to Bryan's. Slow, deliberate, sure. "Yes."

CHAPTER 17

*S*helby peeled her surgical gown off and tossed it in the garbage with her gloves, cap, and mask. She'd stayed to cover when one of the second shift vets was late. After a C-section delivery of five Great Dane puppies, she'd moved straight to emergency surgery for a hemoabdomen on a golden retriever. They'd stopped the internal bleeding and finished up with a transfusion to help with blood loss.

Thankfully, both patients appeared likely to make a full recovery, and the puppies were all doing well, too. But it was now nearly six p.m., and she was exhausted after eleven hours on her feet. Exhausted and ready to go home where she could fall into bed.

With Dev, preferably.

With less clothes even more preferably.

Her pulse sped up as she headed for the door. She'd managed to focus when needed, but all it took was one glimpse of him to recall how safe and warm and amazing it felt to be held in his arms last night. Would he offer the comfort of his bed again tonight, or expect her to man up?

Maybe the better question was, should she attempt to be strong, or use the situation to her advantage? The idea of that felt wrong, and yet being close to him had felt so right.

When she pushed through the door, she was surprised to see Reyes still in the hall with his brother. "What are you still doing here?"

"It's two Torrezes for the price of one," he joked.

"Lucky me." She grinned while glancing at the orange folder Dev had closed the moment she'd stepped through the doors. "I wasn't complaining, you know, just figured you'd have gone home hours ago."

"Dev and I were catching up on things. Plus, it was cool to see you in action. I must say, I'm super impressed."

She shrugged lightly, her curiosity over the folder growing. "Just doing my job."

It was more than that, and his return smile confirmed he understood it was more of a passion considering they both knew she didn't need to work.

"You do it well," Reyes said. "Don't know that I'll ever be able to call you Baby Bells again now that I've seen you all grown up."

"Thank God for that," she exclaimed with a laugh. "Especially since I've been grown up for years."

He turned a grin toward his brother. "Funny, that's what Dev said the other day."

"Oh really?" She switched her gaze to the man responsible for the butterflies tickling her stomach. "How ironic, considering he treats me like a kid."

Dev's arched brow challenged her words in a way that had those butterfly wings fluttering faster.

"Fine, you've been better," she admitted with a small smile. To be fair, ever since she'd called him on it Sunday night, he had been *much* better. Especially considering she'd been too chicken to be alone any longer than it took for a quick shower.

To change the subject, she pointed toward the folder in his hand. "What do you have there?"

"Work stuff."

It was her turn to arch her brows. "Far as I know, *I'm* your work. So, what is it?"

He shook his head and lightly tapped the folder against his leg. "Not now. You ready to go home?"

The curt shut-down morphed her butterflies to anxiety. A glance at Reyes gave her nothing. Whatever it was, Dev didn't want to talk about it. Or he didn't want to talk to *her* about it.

Resentment stiffened her spine. So much for being straight with her. She was about to remind him of his promise when his other words from that day came back to her: *Trust me.*

Take a breath, Shelby.

Okay. She'd assume he had a good reason for keeping the information to himself. For now, anyway.

Lifting her chin to meet his gaze, she said, "Yeah, I'm ready."

He gave her a brief nod, a glimmer of thanks in his blue-green eyes telling her he appreciated her not pushing the subject. Her tension eased, and she went to retrieve her purse from her locker in the break room.

Before they parted ways with Reyes in the parking lot,

she stepped forward to give him a hug. "Thanks again for staying with me today."

She'd felt as equally protected with him as with Dev, and was grateful she'd been able to spend the day focusing on work, not her personal life.

"Anytime. Stay safe," he whispered in her ear before letting go and heading out.

Dev was quiet as he drove, and Shelby began to wonder if this was going to be how the rest of the evening went when they got home.

Home?

No. She had to be more careful. He could call it home, but for her, it was Dev's house.

Finally, she couldn't stand the silence anymore. "How'd your appointments go?"

He lifted a shoulder while doing a round of checking the mirrors. "Gus and the police are still working on things."

Shelby ducked her chin to see the passenger side mirror even as she noted he wasn't taking a circuitous route this time. "So, nothing new?"

"Not yet."

Then why had he stuffed that folder behind his seat instead of setting it between them where she could've reached over to check it out? He'd said, *"Not now,"* in the hospital, but even with just the two of them in his truck, clearly, he wasn't going to willingly volunteer any information.

As she watched the car behind them for the past mile or so make a right turn, it took conscious effort not to grind her teeth. Man, she couldn't wait for this all to be over. To be able to drive herself somewhere. No more being escorted. No more being afraid of every shadow. No more people telling her only what they thought she could handle.

No more—

No more Dev.

At least, no more Dev as she'd gotten used to. The moment the stalker was caught, her time with him would be over.

A sharp ache tightened her chest as he turned into his driveway.

Once they were inside, he reactivated the security system, and she waited by the door while he did a quick recon of the house. Tension gripped her muscles until he returned from the bedrooms and gave her a swift, reassuring smile.

"All clear. I've got some stuff to bring in from my truck, but first I'll get dinner started."

Shelby grimaced as she toed off her tennis shoes and moved into the living room. "What if we have something delivered? I just want to take a shower and veg out."

"Go ahead. You don't have to help."

She watched him head to the kitchen, turning to follow his movements. It wasn't a big deal, and yet it didn't seem right to leave him to do all the work.

He glanced up after taking a number of items from the fridge and setting them on the counter. "Take a load off while you can, Shelby. Because after dinner, I'm putting you to work."

"Doing dishes?"

"Nope."

She arched her brows in question.

Dev shook his head, keeping the secret as he reached

for a cutting board. "Go. I'll let you know when dinner is ready."

She went, and was halfway through her shower when she realized he'd left the folder in his truck. Was that what he had to get yet? Was that what they'd be working on after dinner? She turned to rinse the conditioner from her hair and closed her eyes as the hot water streamed over her body.

A tilt of her head and slight angling of her body had the water hitting the part of her shoulder between her neck and shoulder blade. What she really needed was a nice, firm massage. The thought of asking Dev to put his strong, warm hands on her skin sent a flash of heat from head to toe.

Seduce that man.

Raine's suggestion sent another spear of heat much deeper. It lingered as she dried off and dressed. If her time with Dev was limited, she should make the most of the time she did have left. While she wasn't nearly brave enough to dig the negligee from her suitcase, she did pick out her most clingy T-shirt with a low V-neck, and a pair of curve-hugging, hot-pink velvet lounge shorts that barely covered her butt.

Nerves tickled her stomach as she left her bedroom, even as the smell of chicken and spices had her mouth watering. Sounds from the empty fourth bedroom brought her to the doorway to find Dev unwrapping plastic from a section of gym mat he then lay next to another section already on the floor. One more to go, and the entire surface would be covered.

He shot her a glance, then did a double take, his gaze sliding from her damp, braided hair to her bare feet.

"What's this?" she asked as her whole body flushed with heat from that one look.

He turned away and ripped the plastic from the last mat. "This is for after dinner."

Confusion prompted a smile of bewilderment. "Are you going to make me do yoga? Gymnastics? Wrestling?"

A smile tugged at his mouth with all her guesses while he placed the last section. "I'm not going to make you do anything. But I am going to give you back some control."

She eyed the cushioned floor with a frown. "How so?"

"I'm going to teach you self-defense."

CHAPTER 18

*D*ev had a good half-dozen bites to go, and Shelby was already up at the sink rinsing her plate. He'd been a little nervous about his plan, but the moment he'd said *self-defense,* her eyes had lit up. She wolfed down her chicken stir-fry and rice and was raring to go.

Now, he was dragging his feet. Because how the fuck was he supposed to concentrate on teaching her when all he could think about was touching her? Every tempting, tantalizing, deliciously-scented inch of her.

He'd about swallowed his tongue when she'd appeared in the doorway after her shower—because imagining her under the steamy spray wasn't bad enough. Under that tight gray T-shirt, he could see the faint outline of her dark bra. And those hot pink short shorts. They were just begging him to run his palm up her bare thigh to the curve of her ass cheek. He was dying to compare the velvet of the material to the velvet of her skin.

Clearly, after crossing the line last night when he

allowed himself to touch her in the name of comfort, there was no going back. That fact had been obvious when he'd come up with this plan requiring all kinds of body contact and hadn't even tried to reason himself out of it. At least by teaching her self-defense, he could pretend it was for an altruistic reason.

You know, idiot, you might just end up giving her the courage to sleep alone again.

That was the point, wasn't it? Keeping her safe and making sure she *felt* safe was all part of the job. Even if the end result meant she didn't need him tonight, boosting her confidence was more important.

Shelby paced back to the couch from the kitchen. "You eat like my Grandpa Ira," she complained.

"You don't want to start the second you're done eating," he reasoned. "You need to let your food settle."

"It's not like swimming."

"You won't be saying that when you throw up."

"Okay, fine." She perched on the edge of the cushions and gave him a sheepish smile. "I can't help it. I'm a little excited."

"Only a little?" he teased, even though her eagerness made his heart happy. It felt good to give her something back instead of only telling her what she couldn't do.

"I don't know why *I* didn't think of something like this sooner," she mused.

Dev shot her a sideways glance. "From what I saw today, you're busy at work, and you've got more than enough going on with family, too. All those weddings and babies."

"There is that," she agreed, sitting back on the couch while he finished eating. "Not that I'm complaining.

Family-wise, it's been a great year. It'll be nice when I can babysit again."

Which wouldn't be until her stalker was caught. A brief wish that it didn't happen too soon brought a huge wave of guilt. Because now that he'd crossed that line, selfishness was beginning to creep in. He ate his last bite and rose to take his plate to the kitchen.

Shelby twisted around and draped her elbow over the back of the couch. "How long will it take you to teach me?"

"Depends on how fast you pick it up." He shrugged while rinsing his dish. "Could be a couple of nights, or a couple of weeks. The most important thing will be practicing so the moves become automatic if you need them."

"And you really think I can learn it?"

"I saw you give a dog a C-section today. I *know* you can learn to kick some ass."

He looked up to see her smile as she watched him, but the moment their gazes met, she dropped her attention to where she was tracing the seam of the couch with her thumbnail.

"So…um…if this guy is caught before we're done, will you keep teaching me?"

"Of course." The reply was automatic, but no less sincere. And the relief in the return of her smile made his pulse skip in a way that had him equally dreading and anticipating the next hour. He walked past the couch toward the hall. "Let's go."

She popped up to follow him. "Don't you need to let your food settle?"

"I'm used to eating and getting right back to physical work."

"Because of the military?"

"Right." He picked up the training suit he'd bought with the mats. "But enough talk. Let's get to it."

Her head tilted as she watched him gear up in all the pads. A smile tugged at her mouth. "You need all that for little 'ole me?"

He flashed back to the stairwell incident at the hospital. "Considering how well-acquainted I am with your knee—yep."

Her smirk became a grimace. "I apologized for that."

"Though you didn't have to. You did good. I got this because I don't want you to pull your punches. You need to practice as if it's the real deal, and that means hitting me as hard as you can."

A small frown furrowed her brow.

He held the padded helmet against his hip. "First lesson, though, is to use your voice. If you're attacked, yell as loud as you can to intimidate your attacker and draw attention if anyone is nearby. You yell, and you keep yelling until you're safe."

She nodded.

"Next, always go for the four most vulnerable areas. Eyes, nose, throat, and—"

"Groin?" she finished with another smirk.

He gave her a mock glare. "You didn't have to apologize, but that doesn't mean you get to laugh at my pain."

"Sorry." She straightened, making a show of wiping the humor from her expression.

Which had him fighting a smile when he needed them both to take this seriously.

"We're going to start with the hammer strike. When you're alone, walking to or from your vehicle, have your keys ready in your hand, and strike at your attacker like swinging a hammer." He demonstrated the stance and motion, then put on the helmet to advance on her. "For right now, just make a fist and hit me."

Shelby got in a tentative stance and when he was close enough, reached out to tap her fist against his helmet.

"What was that?" he demanded. "Where's your voice?"

She arched her brows. "In here?"

"Anywhere," he barked. "And *hit* me. As hard as you can. That's what the padding is for."

She frowned and nodded at the same time.

"Let's go again."

Even before she was in her stance, he lunged at her. She squeaked and swung. The hit was better, but, "You sounded like a mouse. A meek little mouse. Is that what you are?"

Her eyes were wide as they met his. "No."

"Then yell and fucking hit me. Do you need me to put on a red shirt? Or better yet, tell you how I can't wait to see *you* in red?"

Her brown eyes narrowed, and when he went for her this time, she yelled and struck out like she was swinging a ten pound hammer with everything she had. Then she jumped back with a gasp, both hands flying up to cover her mouth.

"Much better. Again."

She gave a hesitant smile at his praise, then went serious again. After a few more reps, her hesitation melted away, and her confidence bloomed.

Dev moved on to the palm heel strike. When he explained how to jam the heel of her palm up toward his nostrils or under his chin to jar his jaw, her frown returned.

"Won't that hurt?" she asked as she pantomimed his moves in the air.

"That's the point."

"I don't want to hurt you."

"We don't train with these suits in Special Forces, and I sparred with guys twice your size on a regular basis. You can't hurt me any worse than they did." He shifted to her right. "I'm going to come at you from the side this time. Get in front of me as much as you can before you strike."

She nodded and got ready. With a slight glance over her shoulder, she asked, "Do you miss it?"

"Getting the shit beat out of me?"

Her lips curved in a smile. "I highly doubt you got the shit beat out of you, but no, I meant the military. Do you—"

He attacked, and she pivoted, planted her feet, and yelled loud enough to make his ears ring while jamming her heel up under his chin hard enough to snap his head back.

"Wow. Nice."

"So, do you?" she persisted as she reset.

Exertion had elevated her breathing, and as his gaze strayed to her chest in that tight T-shirt, he forgot what she was talking about.

Eyes up, man. Focus. Do you miss the military? "Yeah. I do."

"Would you go back if you could?"

The question made him pause. A month ago, he'd have answered yes without hesitation. Right now, with her in front of him, it wasn't an automatic reply. Not like earlier, when she asked if he'd keep teaching her if the stalker was caught before they finished.

Without a way to explain the unexpected *no* forming in his head, he said shortly, "I can't go back, so it's a moot point."

Also, a month ago, he was still pissed off at the abrupt end to his career. He'd been floundering, wondering what the fuck he was going to do with the rest of his life. Now, he saw a glimmer of potential for something he hadn't imagined before.

Protective services. Training. He could continue to help keep people safe like he had in the Special Forces, just with more preventative measures than rescues after the fact.

Before she could ask more unsettling questions, he moved on to the groin kick, and finished their first lesson with how to escape the bear hug attack. She was a quick study and could execute each move fairly smooth after a good dozen reps.

"All right, that's it for tonight." Not only did she look exhausted, but the bear hug attacks had his senses drowning in the scent of whatever fruity body wash or shampoo she'd used in her shower. Thank God for padding. "You did great for the first lesson."

"Really?"

The hopeful lilt to her voice had him giving her a smile of reassurance as he peeled off the suit. "Really. Tomorrow we can practice all these again, and I'll add a few more."

"Any chance we can try a few without the suit right now?"

Fuck. He turned to lay the padding against the wall

with a silent groan. The distance it had afforded him was the only reason he'd made it this far.

"I just want to see what it's like without the padding," Shelby added. "So it feels more real."

Feeling her was precisely the problem.

"Yeah. Sure." Because of course, he'd been having trouble saying no to her since the night of the wedding.

She did great with her hammer and palm heel strikes, even if he could tell she was holding back. He didn't argue that for tonight.

"We're going to skip the groin kicks for now," he advised, and she laughed.

A second later, when she turned her back, he seized the opportunity to catch her off guard and grabbed her from behind in the bear hug. It might have also been that he didn't want to give himself a chance to over-think how close the move would bring him without the suit.

He should've given himself the chance to think about it.

Should've prepared mentally for the feel of her ass snugged up tight against his groin. The soft cushion of her full breasts against his forearms. Heat spread like wildfire until she let out a yell and bent at the waist to drop her weight. Next thing he knew, she rotated her upper body to slam her elbow up into his jaw on the right, then the left, and back to the right.

Muscle memory kicked in from hand to hand combat training, and he was able to pull back just enough to avoid a sore jaw in the morning. Her hip swivel twisted her free of his arms, and she reached up to pull his head down while lifting her knee toward his groin.

Pure instinct had him jerking back, and his weight

shift at the odd angle tweaked his knee. The searing stab of pain dropped him to the mat with an involuntary grunt.

Shelby gasped and dropped to her knees to lean over him. "Oh my God. I'm so sorry. Are you okay?"

"I'm fine," he said through gritted teeth. Or he would be, as soon as she wasn't leaning over him, her beautiful brown eyes swimming with concern as she worried the corner of her bottom lip with her teeth.

Her palms rested on his chest, and when her gaze met his from less than a foot away, she suddenly froze. A flare of heat thickened the air, and he reached to grasp her arms to set her away. Only, once his palms made contact with her bare skin, all he could think about was pulling her closer.

Her attention slid to his mouth, and his name came out on a whisper of breath. "Dev."

When her tongue darted out to wet her lips, he was a goner.

With a low groan of defeat, he dragged her in. She might have met him halfway, but the instant their lips melded, he was swept along on a tsunami of desire a decade in the making.

Her lips were silky soft, and her breathy little moan parted them just enough for him to slide his tongue in for a taste. She opened for him, and he took full advantage to stroke deeper. So sweet. Hot. And the way she met him stroke for stroke was addicting in a way that had him rolling her over, using her momentum to keep them going until he lay on top of her.

Well, partially on top—with his swelling erection

pressed firmly against her thigh, right about where those pink velvet shorts kissed the curve of her ass cheek.

She slid her hands from his chest, up around his neck to rake her nails through his hair. The smile she tilted up from beneath her lashes was a contradiction of shyness and pure siren. Just like that day in her bedroom all those years ago when she'd offered him her innocence.

He stilled as desire battled with honor. Many things had changed in nine years, but his reason for saying no back then was the same reason he had to say no now.

His first duty was to protect her.

CHAPTER 19

Shelby felt Dev pulling away before he actually moved. She saw the regret in his eyes and tried to keep him from leaving her. But she was no match for his strength as he pushed up from the mat. Away from her.

"I can't," he bit out, his tone gruff and angry. "I'm sorry."

"I don't understand." She lay there blinking up at him, weighed down by crushing hurt and disappointment.

"Don't look at me like that. I have to be responsible, Shelby."

He reached out a hand to help her up. She frowned at the gesture, but gripped his fingers before the thought of refusing fully formed. Apparently, she'd take any excuse to touch him.

He tugged free and turned away the moment she was on her feet.

Hurt stabbed again, followed by resentment. "How is kissing me irresponsible?"

When he kept heading for the door, she followed and raised her voice. "The least you can do is answer me."

Dev swung around so fast she jerked back in surprise.

His gaze bored into hers, dark and angry. "It's irresponsible because when I was kissing you, I wasn't thinking of anything else but burying myself deep inside you and the hell with the rest of the world." Heat flared in his eyes, and he clenched his jaw. "I have to stay aware."

The blunt words had her heart pounding so hard it nearly knocked the wind out of her. "Isn't that why you have the security system?"

A fierce frown darkened his expression. "No, Shelby. I did not install security so I could fuck around on the job like your other useless bodyguard."

"That's not what I meant," she protested.

"You are *my* responsibility," he ground out as he jabbed his thumb into his chest. "Your safety has to be my number one priority. I can't get complacent while this bastard is still out there. If something happened to you because I wasn't good enough—" He abruptly snapped his mouth shut. His gaze held hers for another heart-thumping second, and then he spun back to the door. "I can't let my guard down for a second. Neither should you."

She didn't try to stop him as she sucked a deep breath into tight lungs. A whole kaleidoscope of emotions had her reeling. She'd been kissed before, but never like that. Like he wanted to devour her. The throb of his arousal against her leg had triggered an answering pulse of need deep inside.

Need that currently had her fighting the urge to go after him. But those telling words just before he'd snapped his mouth shut shed a ray of light on his confusing surges of anger. She'd always assumed he was mad at her, but now she wondered if it was directed at himself. Was he really that worried he wasn't good enough to do the job?

Maybe he needed her as much as she needed him. Needed to know she trusted him—with her life—and had every confidence in his ability to keep her safe.

When she ventured from the room, she was surprised to realize it was after nine p.m. Dev was at his dresser in his bedroom, and she hovered in the doorway.

"You okay if I still sleep in here tonight?"

"I figured you would."

That didn't really answer her question, did it? Still, since it wasn't an outright no, she didn't question further before brushing her teeth and returning to slip beneath the covers. He took his turn in the bathroom, then shut off the light before getting into bed.

Shelby took a breath to speak at the exact moment he shifted onto his side, facing away from her. Pressing her lips together, she kept the words inside, hands folded over the comforter across her stomach.

It felt like she lay there for hours, staring up at the dark ceiling. In reality, it was probably more like five or ten minutes before she finally whispered, "Dev?"

No answer.

"You still awake?"

A grunt from his side of the bed held a note of annoyance.

That kept her quiet for another few minutes, until under the cover of darkness, she found the courage to ask the question she'd agonized over for so long. "You had nothing to protect me from that day in my bedroom, so why did you react the way you did?"

"I had plenty to protect you from," he growled.

"Like what? You just left," she accused. "As if I didn't matter to you at all."

He turned his head in the dark, then rolled over onto his back. "You mattered, Shelby."

"Didn't seem like it when I didn't see you again for nine years." Old emotions tangled with new to clog her voice. "We used to be friends."

"Walking away from you was the hardest thing I've ever done," he admitted gruffly.

"Then why did you?"

"I was twenty-one. You were only sixteen."

"I was old enough," she defended. "All my friends were having sex already."

"Worst reason *ever* to have sex," he retorted.

He was right about that. Even more so because she'd only had one close friend back then. And her cousin, Raine.

How about because I loved you?

Nope, not asking that question.

"It was the only way I knew to protect you," he said quietly.

"Walking out of my life and not talking to me again was protecting me?"

"That was right after I'd graduated Special Forces training, you remember?"

She nodded, then quickly added, "Yes."

"I was given one week of leave before I had to go back for my first mission. How could I be with you knowing I couldn't make any promises about coming back? Out of respect for you, and your parents, your whole family, I had to walk away."

"You could have explained that to me instead of yelling like you did."

"I was angry, Shelby. At the situation—and at you. Offering yourself to me like you did was reckless and naïve, and right or wrong, I wanted to scare you, maybe even shame you, into not going to someone else. Apparently, *that* didn't work."

She frowned at his tight tone, until she remembered that day in her dad's office when she'd purposely taunted him. Guilt prompted her to admit, "It did, actually."

From the corner of her eye, she saw the shadow of his head roll toward her on his pillow.

"I lied when I said you were a practice run. I only wanted you." That last came out as a whisper, and the following *I still only want you* was gulped back with a wave of nerves.

"It took every ounce of mental training I had to resist you that day."

Hearing the sincerity in his voice, going over his words and why he'd rejected her, her hurt eased for the first time in years. "And all this time I thought it was that you didn't want me."

He gave a wry grunt and turned back toward the ceiling. "Nothing could be further from the truth. Then or now."

Her pulse skipped at that last bit. "I'm sorry I was mad at you about it for so long. I'm sorry what I did drove you away and kept you out of my life for so long. I don't want that to happen again."

"I'm sorry, too," he said. "For how I handled it, and for hurting you."

She squeezed her eyes tight against the burn of tears as emotion swelled in her chest. It gently eased, giving way for an unexpected sense of peace. "You know how I didn't want you to take this job at first?"

"Yeah." There was a smile in his voice.

"I'm really glad you did. I trust you to keep me safe more than anyone else. And I'm not saying that to add pressure on you, I just want you to know, I'm glad it's you who's got my back."

After a long moment of silence, suddenly his hand covered hers. She sucked in a breath as her heart fluttered high in her throat. He threaded his fingers with hers and then laid their joined hands in the space on the bed between them.

She heard his hard swallow, and the slightly shaky cadence of his breathing. His grip tightened briefly, but he didn't say anything else or try to touch her in any other way. And for now, the unspoken thanks was more than enough to secure his place in her heart for the rest of her life.

CHAPTER 20

*I*t was still dark the next morning when Dev eased out of bed at five a.m. and started a pot of coffee. Then he retrieved the folder from where he'd stashed it last night in a lower kitchen cupboard.

He'd reviewed about half of the letters with Reyes while waiting for Shelby to finish her extended shift yesterday, but he wanted to go over the rest—hopefully before she got up. And if she did, well, the death threats weren't something he wanted her to see, but he wouldn't keep them from her if she asked again.

Stirring a teaspoon of sugar into his coffee while standing at the counter, he slid the folder closer while recalling those moments in bed with Shelby the night before. He hadn't outright lost it since losing Gonzales on a mission in Syria five years ago—not even last November when he'd realized his injury would end his career.

But last night, when she voiced her faith in him, he'd been too choked up to do anything more than hold her

168

hand in gratitude. She'd fallen asleep shortly after, and her even, relaxed breathing had lulled him along with her.

Not long ago, he'd told himself he was lucky he hadn't done something as stupid as fall for her all those years ago. But he'd been lying to himself. He'd loved her then, and loved her even more so now. He'd managed to not give in after that inferno of a kiss, but as soon as he was no longer her bodyguard, all bets were off.

Speaking of which, he refocused his attention and opened the folder to flip though to where he and Rey had left off. Shelby's phone alarm sounded faintly from the bedroom about six, and by then Dev had marked two letters in particular he wanted the PI to look into further.

She shuffled out in her slippers a few minutes later, sleepy-eyed with her hair slightly mussed. Cute and sexy all at once.

He closed the folder and tucked it away before turning to pour her a cup of coffee. Then he slid it and the container of sea salt caramel hot chocolate she'd brought from her place across the island as she slumped down onto one of the stools.

"Thanks." She dumped a heaping scoop of hot chocolate into her cup and stirred. "I slept like a rock."

Good. He loved knowing she felt safe enough for that. "You had a long day yesterday."

"Thank God I'm not on the surgery floor today," she mumbled before blowing across the surface of her cup and taking a sip.

When she gave a closed-eyed *hmm* of pleasure, Dev had to look away. A quickly snuck glance caught sight of her tongue flicking out to catch the drip on her bottom lip, and he wished he could be the one to lean over and lick it off.

He turned away to top off his half-empty cup.

"How long have you been up?" she asked.

Since about five seconds ago, and half the night before that.

He thumped the coffee pot back on the burner and attempted casual by leaning back against the cupboard. "About an hour."

"Still those military hours?"

He smiled slightly, because it was close enough.

She took another sip before straightening in her chair, her expression suddenly determined. "What was the deal with that folder yesterday? I meant to ask you about it last night, but you distracted me with the self-defense."

"You don't miss much, do you?"

"Nope."

Dev sighed and brought the folder back out. He stepped forward and placed it on the counter, but kept his palm on the top when she reached for it. "This is only because I promised to be straight with you."

"And I appreciate that." She gripped the edge between her thumb and forefinger and tugged.

He kept his hold. "These are copies of death threats and other borderline letters sent to your dad."

She stopped pulling, her brown gaze somber as it rose to his.

"The choice is yours, but I don't think you should read them. They're not...nice."

"What death threat is?"

He let go of the folder and watched closely as she opened it to read the top letter. Emotions chased across her face and left a deep crease in her forehead. She flipped to the second page, but slammed the whole thing closed about five seconds later. A quick shove of her hand spun the folder back in his direction.

"God, people can be so horrible." She was still frowning as she took a gulp of her coffee. "I knew he got stuff like that, but didn't know how bad it was. *Is.*"

"I'm sure your parents don't want you to worry about them. And they're not all as bad as those top ones. Ninety-nine-point-nine-nine percent of the time it's just idiots venting their anger."

"Yeah, but all it takes is that point-o-one percent to be more than an idiot blowing off steam, doesn't it?"

"That's why your parents have their own protection."

She nodded, then sought his gaze once more. "Why do you have these letters?"

"Gus was going through them to see if there could be any connection to whoever's been bothering you. I offered to be a second pair of eyes."

"And?"

Even though he'd promised to tell her everything, he still hesitated. After seeing her reaction to just a couple of the threats, he worried that admitting he saw the possibility of two connections would magnify her anxiety.

She watched him over the rim of her cup as she took a sip. "You found something, didn't you?"

"Maybe," he reluctantly admitted. "I was going to call Gus to see if he saw the same thing and have him check it out."

Her gaze flicked down to the folder, and after a moment, she squared her shoulders. "Which one?" When he didn't move right away, she reasoned, "If the connection is to me, maybe I can confirm it."

He sighed slightly, then located one of the letters toward the back that had stood out the most and passed it over.

Her gaze skimmed back and forth, her frown returning as she read out loud, "'Until you lose a child, you can never fully understand the responsibility you have to do what's right for the survivors. It is our duty as parents to protect our children. You must advocate for them, or you will be replaced with someone who will.'" She sat back and stared at the paper. "It's so articulate. Not like the other one where every other word was a swear word."

"Yeah. Those—and most of the others—generally tend to be the hotheads blowing off steam. It's the present-tense wording that elevates it from implied to actual threat. In my opinion anyway."

Her eyes narrowed as she leaned in to look closer again. "When was it sent?"

"It's older—from right after your dad became governor."

"That was six years ago."

"I still want to have Gus look further into who sent it —if he hasn't already."

"Surely it would've been dealt with by now?" she asked.

"Everything in that folder has been investigated by either the Colorado police, or the Capitol police, and prosecuted as needed. But it's the wording that caught my attention."

"*Until you've lost a child*?"

"Yeah. The man's daughter was killed in a shooting a year before he sent the letter."

Shelby frowned. "That's horrible."

"It is," Dev agreed. "And he was determined not to be a threat at the time, but with your dad's strong stance on the second amendment and everything heating up on gun control laws, maybe it's got the guy stewing again and looking for someone to blame. Or for revenge. Or to make your dad understand by going after one of his kids."

Not to mention, all the little incidences with Shelby had started suspiciously close to the anniversary of the daughter's death.

She stared into her cup in silence.

"I'm not saying that to scare you, I just want you to be aware."

After one last drink, Shelby slid off the stool while setting her cup down. "I'll make sure I'm done with work on time today so we can get in double time on the self-defense." An arch of her eyebrows followed. "If you're good with that?"

Approval surged forward as he nodded.

That's my girl. Don't back down.

CHAPTER 21

$\mathcal{A}$bout an hour before Shelby's shift ended later that afternoon, Dev set his magazine aside and hurried to hold the hospital clinic door open for a petite, older woman hobbling in on crutches with her left foot in a boot.

Her blue eyes crinkled at the corners as she smiled her appreciation. "Thank you."

"Of course."

"I didn't know the clinic had gotten themselves a door-man. What a classy touch."

Dev smiled that she thought he was a doorman in his boots, jeans, and unzipped black fleece jacket over a black T-shirt. But he didn't correct her—no sense alarming an old lady.

With no animal in sight, he asked, "Are you picking up?"

"My grandson is parking the car. He'll bring Pixie in with him in just a moment."

Dev glanced back in time to see a guy step back from a

pearl white Cadillac SUV as a large black and tan Rottweiler jumped down from the back seat.

Pixie?

"Mrs. Walters!" Shelby's voice exclaimed. "What did you do? Are you okay?"

Dev turned back to see she'd come through the double doors from the back, her expression concerned as she greeted the older lady.

"Oh, I'm fine. Just twisted my ankle on a patch of ice."

Shelby flicked her gaze to Dev, gave him a quick smile that put a warm glow in his chest, then looked past him as she asked, "Where's Pixie?"

Dev caught the slight falter in her smile and turned to see what caused the reaction. His whole body stiffened at the sight of Chad Mayer on the other end of the Rottweiler's leash.

"There she is now," Mrs. Walters said. "My grandson insisted on chauffeuring me today."

Mayer opened the door, his gaze bouncing between the three of them standing there. Shelby bent as the dog rushed forward, stub of a tail wiggling along with its big, solid butt.

"Hello there, Pixie. How you doing girl?" She gave the dog a rub by the jowls while tilting her head to glance up. "Hey, Chad."

Dev heard the forced smile in her voice and instinctively eased closer. Mayer shot him one more glance before giving her a friendly grin.

"Shelby, hey. I forgot you worked here."

Bullshit.

"You two know each other?" Mrs. Walters asked.

Oh, boy. There was definitely matchmaker's hope in that question.

"We do," Shelby answered, her voice bright and cheerful as she extended her hand for the dog's leash without explaining how. "Let's get Pixie in for her pedicure so I can stay on schedule."

The moment Mayer reached toward her, Dev shot his hand out and took the leash. Giving the guy a stern glare, he passed the leather handle to Shelby.

Mrs. Walters laughed, oblivious to the tension. "Ginny from my bridge group has a huge Golden Doodle with bright pink toenails."

"Oh, my." Shelby straightened and started for the back, her step slow enough for the woman to keep up on her crutches. "Sorry, but we don't do pink here."

When Mayer started after them, Dev stopped him with a hand to his chest, and pointed toward the chairs in the waiting area. "*You* can wait right over there."

The guy stepped back with a frown. "What is your problem?"

"No problem. We're just going to let Bells do her job, and then you can take Grandma and Pixie back home."

A tick flickered near Mayer's eye with Dev's purposeful use of Shelby's nickname. That vibe he'd gotten the first time he saw him twinged harder than ever as Mayer stalked over to take a seat. Dev stood right where he was until Shelby walked Mrs. Walters and Pixie back out a half-hour later. Then he took the leash to pass back to Mayer. No way was he going to let the guy even get close enough to touch her.

After paying her bill, Mrs. Walters made her way toward the exit on her crutches. Shelby stayed behind the counter, and Dev moved ahead to get the door with a conscious effort to not reveal any evidence of his limp.

The woman smiled her appreciation, and then said over her shoulder to Shelby, "Thank you again so much, dear. We'll see you in a couple of months."

"Without the boot," she replied. "Take care of yourself and watch out for ice patches."

"Oh, believe me, I will."

Pixie pulled on her leash to follow, but Mayer held her back long enough to say, "Always good to see you, Shelby."

She smiled, and again, Dev read the discomfort in the tight lines at the corners of her mouth.

The guy was smart enough to follow his grandmother out to her vehicle without another word.

Once the front door was closed, Dev pivoted to join Shelby on her way to the back. "Has he been here before?"

She shook her head. "I didn't even know he was her grandson. Though she did mention having one the last two times."

"I don't like that guy."

A grin curved her mouth as she straightened up the exam room. "Never woulda guessed."

Dev shrugged. Yeah, he might have overdone the bodyguard role, but just the thought of Mayer looking at her the wrong way had him ready to kick his ass.

Shelby braced one hand on the table, the other on her hip. "Anyways, he's gone, and I'm done for the day. Get me out of here before an emergency comes in."

He swept his arm toward the door. "As you wish."

She grabbed her things from the break room, and they walked out to his truck.

"You ready for your next lesson?" he asked.

"Ready and willing."

The eagerness in her voice skipped his mind clear over self-defense, straight to the bedroom. The word *willing* didn't help one damn bit. It had him picturing that sexy little satin slip from back when she was sixteen.

"Although..." At the passenger door, Shelby gave him a head tilt and eyebrow arch that was becoming very familiar. "Isn't there something you wanted to ask me first?"

He paused with his fingers curled around the door handle. "And what would that be?"

"Dinner at your parents'?"

Well, crap. Dev jerked open the door, his jaw tightening. "Mom texted you," he guessed as she climbed inside.

"She did," Shelby confirmed. "And I said—"

He slammed the door on what she said. Because of course, after he'd answered his mom's text about dinner with a *no,* she'd gone behind his back because she knew Shelby would say *yes.*

Her gaze had him tingling with awareness every step of the way around the front of his truck. As soon as he opened the door, she finished her sentence.

"I said yes."

"I thought you wanted to put in extra time on self-defense."

"We can do both," she argued. "I had to switch the vet check with Grayson to tomorrow, but we don't have to be there until ten. So we can work late and sleep in."

"Easy for you to say," he groused as he started the engine and drove toward the exit. "I haven't slept in in over ten years."

She shrugged lightly. "I can always text her back if you want. It's just that I haven't seen them much since moving out of my parents' place, and I thought it would be nice to sit and visit."

And once again, he couldn't say no to Shelby.

After she changed into a pair of skinny jeans and a soft, cream-colored sweater back at his house, they were on their way again—with a detour for dessert at her sister-in-law's bakery, Must Love Frosting.

"I'm shocked Mom asked you to bring anything," he commented. While his mother never went anywhere empty-handed, she also never asked guests to bring anything to her house.

"I insisted," Shelby said. "And I know she loves Honor's tiramisu."

They ended up with the tiramisu, and a half-dozen assorted cupcakes loaded with two inches of buttercream. He eyed the mountain of sugar as he carried the bakery boxes out to his truck. "That's insane."

"Insanely good," she countered. "Have you had one of her cupcakes before?"

"Can't say that I have."

"They're the best. Seriously."

"I'll take your word for it." He handed over the boxes once she was in her seat. "You can get a cavity just looking at one of those things."

"It's worth it," she declared.

Dev shook his head, until he remembered Asher's wife had baked Loyal and Roxanna's wedding cake and yeah, it had been fucking amazing. He'd barely resisted a second piece.

When they reached his parents' house, he knocked first, but didn't wait for them to come to the door before walking in with a loud, "Hello!"

In the next instant, the savory scent of onion and garlic and fresh bread filled his senses. He gave a low groan while taking Shelby's coat to hang with his on the coat tree tucked in the entranceway corner.

"Wow, it smells amazing in here," she said.

"Empanadas," he said with reverence. "I haven't had them in ages."

"I made them just for you, *mijo*."

Dev turned around with a smile. "*Mamá*."

He leaned down to give her a kiss on the cheek and a hug. When she squeezed hard and held on a few extra moments, he was reminded of Shelby's comment the other night about how his mom worried about him and Reyes—and likely Solana, too. A twinge of guilt had him tightening his hold for a brief moment, too. They hadn't made it easy on her or his dad with their profession choices, had they?

Finally his mom let go, and moved to give Shelby a hug. There was a quick exchange of whispers with their smiles, but he chose to ignore it when he heard his mom's heartfelt, "*Thank you.*" He could hardly complain about a little scheming when it got him homemade empanadas and made them both happy.

His dad offered beer or sangria when they all joined him in the kitchen. Shelby took the sangria, but Dev declined. No alcohol for him until the job was done. Instead, he moved to the cupboard to grab a glass for water while his parents returned to their in-tandem cooking. He'd grown up watching them fairly dance together in the kitchen. And then there were the times they literally danced while the sauce simmered.

"Is Rey coming, too?" he asked.

"No." His mom reached up to brush away a dark strand of hair that had escaped the bun at the nape of her neck, her brow furrowed. "He made up some excuse about working on his taxes."

He heard the hurt in her voice, underscored by concern. When he glanced at Shelby leaning against the counter with her glass in hand, she gave him an *I told you* look. He turned back to see his dad graze his mom's arm with his knuckles. She leaned into the gesture as if needing the comfort of his touch.

Dev set his water down and moved up on the other side of his mom. "You don't have to worry, *Mamá.* Rey's working on things, same as me."

She huffed out a breath and twisted to face him, knife in hand. "Of course I worry, Devante. Your father and I both do when you and Reyes hold yourselves at arm's length. Neither of you have been here for family dinner since Christmas, and you're only here tonight because of Shelby."

He shot her another glance, then hung his head with a rough sigh. "You're right, and I'm sorry. I've stayed away because it's not always easy to put on a positive front."

"You don't have to put up a front with us," his mom argued.

"I didn't want you guys to worry."

"It doesn't work that way."

"Yeah, so I've been told."

His mom looked at Shelby, who gave her a quick smile.

When she turned her hopeful expression back up to him, he nodded confirmation before shifting his gaze between her and his dad. "I really am working on things, I promise. You know my physical therapy is going well, and

I also talk to a therapist once a week. I started just before Christmas, and things are going good."

Better than good after this past week. And he'd be great once the danger to Shelby was put behind bars.

His mom dropped the knife and reached up to palm his cheeks with both hands. "Thank you, *mijo.* Please know, you can talk to us anytime. You and Rey. We're here for you always and in anything. That's what family is for."

The tears shimmering in her blue eyes tore at his heart. He reached up to grasp her hands and lowered them between them. "I know you are, but I also need you to understand, there are some things that…you just can't tell the people you love."

"You'll get no judgment from us, Dev," his dad said gruffly. "I would hope you know that."

"I do, Dad, but that's not it." Or maybe it was a little, but not entirely. More so it was to protect them, not himself. "It's…hard to explain. All I can really do is ask you to trust me when I tell you I'm getting the help I need."

His dad nodded.

"And Reyes?" Mom squeezed his hands tight. "Does he talk to someone?"

Dev met his dad's gaze, then shifted back to her with a grimace. "I don't think so. He knows I do, but when I bring it up, he changes the subject, or tells me he's fine."

"Does he talk to you at all?"

"Some."

"Mark tells me he's up all hours of the night whenever they're home," Dad said quietly.

Not quite. Rey could only sleep when he kept the

lights on, but like many things, that was his story to tell. Plus, Dev only knew some of the details.

He gave his mom a gentle smile. "I know it's hard, but we gotta give him time. And I promise, I'll keep working on him."

More tears flooded her eyes as she nodded, and Dev pulled her in for a hug while meeting his dad's gaze over her head. "I'm sorry I didn't talk to you guys sooner. I'll do better."

His dad reached out to give his shoulder a firm squeeze. The glimmer of moisture brightening his eyes made Dev's burn. He quickly blinked the burn away. "So... now that we got through all that, how about we get back to dinner? I heard Shelby's stomach growling on the way over here."

"Oh!" His mom shoved free of his arms and swiped at her cheeks as she gave Shelby a sheepish smile. "Hon, I'm so sorry."

"I'm fine, Elena, really."

Shelby glared at Dev, but having been on the receiving end of more than one of her authentic stare-downs, he didn't buy the fake anger one bit. He grabbed his water glass and made his way over to where she stood while his parents turned their attention back to the food preparation.

"Satisfied?" he asked in reference to the little family therapy session she'd instigated.

She lifted her sangria for a sip while watching the cooks. "The real question is, are you?"

He glanced down when she turned her face up to his. The pride and approval in her soft, brown eyes hit him right in the chest, and his throat constricted as he nodded. "Yeah, I am. Thank you."

"You're welcome."

Her soft smile drew his gaze down to a pair of lips lightly stained from the plum-colored sangria. As he stared, her breath hitched, and her tongue darted out to lick at any stray drops of the fruit-infused wine.

Holy fuck—he wanted his own taste.

When he lifted his gaze to hers, heat sizzled in the air between them, threatening to evaporate every last shred of his common sense.

The creak and thump of the oven door jolted him back to reality. He glanced over to see his mom had pulled out a full pan of empanadas to set on the stovetop, while his dad tossed the Caesar salad.

While taking a breath to try to slow his racing pulse, a light bump of his shoulder against Shelby's sloshed the liquid in her glass. "Come on, help me set the table so we can feed that bear growling in your stomach."

CHAPTER 22

Shelby lifted her arms up over her head as she rolled over, eyes still closed against the inevitable morning after Dev had trained her on more self-defense moves for over an hour after they got back from dinner with his parents.

The soreness in her muscles triggered a low groan with her yawn as she extended her hands outward.

"Hey, whoa, save it for the gym, Slugger."

She gasped at the sound of Dev's gravelly voice from the other side of the bed and jerked her arms back down while whipping her head toward him. "You're still here."

He lifted one arm up behind his head, and left his other resting over his flat stomach as he rolled his head toward her. "Where else would I be?"

"In the kitchen." Seeing him in bed beside her in the light of day had awareness tingling through every cell in her body. "You're always up by now."

"You said I should sleep in."

That's right. Because she was going by Grayson today instead of tomorrow.

"Yeah, I just..." She lost her train of thought when her gaze met his. His eyes were more blue than green in the morning light, and the shadow of stubble darkening his jaw made her want to reach out and feel the rasp of it against her palm. Or her lips.

Realizing she needed to finish her sentence, she quickly said, "I forgot."

"So you weren't trying to smack me on purpose to have the bed to yourself?"

"No," she exclaimed. "Of course not."

His slow smile clued her in he was teasing, and this time she did reach over and smack his arm on purpose—his very firm arm.

He cringed and hunched his shoulder. "Ow."

"Oh please." She rolled her eyes with a grin tugging at her own mouth. "That didn't hurt one bit."

His gaze shifted down to her lips, and his smile faded. From one second to the next, her heart surged up in her throat, making it hard to get enough air into her lungs. It had been two days since that kiss in the makeshift gym, and while she respected his reasons for ending it when he had, she sure as hell wouldn't stop him from kissing her again.

Especially since the past two days had solidified the return of their childhood friendship—just with a heaping dose of sexual tension oozing all over the place.

She shifted under the covers and started to roll onto her side to face him. The loud buzz of his cell vibrating on the nightstand made her jump. Dev blinked, and then whipped his head to the other side of the pillow while grabbing for the phone like it was a lifeline. His quick glance at the screen produced a frown that had Shelby paying attention—especially when he swept the covers aside to sit on the edge of the bed with his back to her.

"Asher. Hey man, what's up?"

What? What the heck was her brother calling Dev for? She pushed into a sitting position and adjusted the hem of her tank top as the covers pooled around her waist.

His voice droned from the phone, but she couldn't make out his words. Dev gave a short, "Yep," and then suddenly sat up straighter, his shoulders rigid. After a moment, he relaxed some, only to tense all over again a minute later. His tone was terse as he nodded and said, "Will do."

Impatience had her tapping him on the shoulder. He shifted toward her on the bed, and his solemn expression made her pulse pick up as she arched her brows in silent expectation.

"Asher—hold up. Shelby's here, so I'm switching you to speaker." After pressing the button, he rested his forearm on his knee to hold the phone out between them. "Go ahead."

"Morning, Bells."

"Hi." She watched Dev's face, but his shuttered expression gave nothing away as she asked, "What's going on?"

"There was a break-in at Mom and Dad's early this morning."

Shelby's stomach lurched. "In D.C.?" The death threat she'd read yesterday against her dad flashed in her head, sending a cold flood of fear down her spine. "Are they okay?"

"They're fine," he assured her. "It wasn't there, it was at the house here in Colorado."

"Thank God there was no one as home." Then it dawned on her he'd said morning, and she sought Dev's gaze. "Elena wasn't there, was she? Is she okay?"

"It happened shortly before she got to work," Asher said. "About six-forty-five. The security company had the police notified and at the house in five minutes."

Good Lord, what time was it? She angled her head to see the time in the upper left hand corner of the screen. *7:45a.m.* Wow, they really had slept in.

"Did they catch the person?" she asked.

"No. They're—"

His voice cut out as Dev's phone beeped for an incoming call. The screen flashed Reyes' name and number.

"You guys still there?"

"We're here," Dev said. "Rey is calling, probably to fill me in. I'll call him back."

"All right." The sound of a blinker came from the microphone as Asher added, "I'm just turning in by Mom and Dad's. I'll let him know if I see him up at the house."

"Thanks."

"Let me know if you find out anything else," Shelby requested. "I can't believe people have the nerve to break-in when it's already light out."

"Bells, I called Dev because I talked to Dad already."

"Okay..." His ominous tone had her searching out Dev's gaze again. Her stomach tightened at the solemn intensity in his expression as her brother continued.

"Based on what they found, the cops said it doesn't appear to be a burglary. I'll look around some, but Mom and Dad will have to give the final word on that when they get back either tonight or tomorrow."

"What exactly did the cops find?" she asked.

Asher hesitated, then gave a heavy sigh. "There was a rose and a bullet left on the end of the bed in both your room and Celia's."

Another chill skittered down her spine. "A rose and a bullet? What the heck does that mean?"

"There was also a note in your room that said, 'Make the right choice.'"

She frowned as the word *choice* struck a memory she couldn't quite grasp.

"With both Shelby and Celia's rooms targeted, it's looking more and more like this is political and aimed at your Dad," Dev said. "Mark told me a major gun bill was coming up for a vote this week. He's been getting a lot of pressure from activists to change his stance."

"Yep," her brother agreed. "Dad's thinking the same thing, and the vote is today. That's why he's not on the way home already."

Shelby shook her head, jaw set. "Dad won't change his vote—at least he better not."

"I think we both know Dad better than that. He's already got someone on the way to Celia's office for protection until this person is caught."

"Good." All of a sudden, the memory teasing the edge of her conscious materialized. Her eyes widened as she made the connection. "Dev—the note on my car at the hospital. It said *one choice made the opposite way can be the difference between life and death.* It's gotta be the same person."

He tilted his head slightly, as if considering the possibility.

"Listen guys," Asher interrupted. "I'm sitting here in the driveway, so I'm going to let you go and get inside."

Dev dropped his gaze to the screen. "Keep us updated."

"Will do. You keep her safe."

"You know I will."

"Love you, Bells."

"Love you, too," she said before Dev disconnected the call while rising and heading over to his dresser.

Shelby swept the covers off her lap to swing her legs over the edge of the bed. "Do you think it could be the same person?"

"Probably," he agreed as he grabbed clean clothes for the day. Shooting her a grimace over his shoulder, he asked, "Any chance I can convince you to lay low for the day?"

Only if you lay with me.

As soon as the thought entered her head, she got up and spun around to make the bed so he wouldn't see the heat warming her cheeks. "I'm not going to let this person imprison me more than I already am."

"Figured you'd say that."

Something in his tone had her looking up as she moved around to straighten his side of the bed. "You think I should just hide for the day?"

His somber gaze met hers across the room. "Do you trust me to keep you safe?"

"Absolutely."

"Then we're going to do whatever you want to do today."

A smile of thanks faded as she thumped his pillow into

place. "Except, it suddenly dawns on me that trusting you to keep me safe also means trusting you to know what's best. So you tell *me* what I'm doing today."

He turned all the way around, clothes in hand as he leaned against his dresser. "Wow. I'm impressed."

She lifted a shoulder, taking the opportunity to drink him in as he stood there in his T-shirt and briefs, his hair all mussed from sleep.

"You said you normally do the vet checks for Grayson on Fridays, right?"

"Always. I only switched to a Thursday because he's got some meeting out of town tomorrow, and seeing him is half the reason I go."

"Then since it's a schedule switch someone wouldn't be expecting, I'm okay with sticking with it."

"You're sure?"

"I am." He headed for the hall. "I'll do a quick security check, then we can both get ready and get going. While you're doing your thing with the dogs, I'll give Gus a call."

Shelby gathered clean clothes to change in the bathroom. The sappy, lovelorn teenager in her wished Dev had insisted they stay home. But that was quickly eclipsed by independence, and the refusal to let fear limit her life. Especially when she had Dev at her side.

CHAPTER 23

ev ended up waiting patiently while Shelby took the time to call her sister and make sure she was okay. Then she called her dad to tell him she wanted him to vote based on the principles he'd campaigned on and been elected for, and nothing else.

Her support for her father despite the possible danger to herself raised his respect to a whole new level. Not only was she still sweet and kind and generous, but she was proving to be a determined fighter who wouldn't be swayed from a fierce belief of right and wrong.

It was nearly an hour later when he pulled into the parking lot of the Cole-Diamond Foundation. Shelby directed him around to the back of the large complex, toward a building with fenced in dog runs off the side. He made a mental note of the layout while sweeping his gaze over the main building that had been built the previous year, surrounded by extensive grounds and some outdoor physical training equipment.

The Diamond fortune being put to good use.

The building he parked in front of featured a prominent sign with the silhouette of a German Shepherd, and the name *Remy's Regiment*.

Shelby grabbed her vet bag from the back seat and waited for him to lead the way inside.

A tall, built black guy looked up from the front desk. He straightened to what had to be at least six-foot-six while offering Dev a polite smile. The moment he spotted Shelby, his eyes lit up and a wide grin spread across his face.

"Hey, girl. What the heck are you doing here today?"

"Change of plans, Eli. How are you this morning?"

"You know me. Always good, but even better now."

He came around the counter, and when it became evident the guy was going in for a hug, Dev stepped between them with a scowl.

Shelby caught his arm. "Dev—Eli's good. He served with Grayson."

He held her back with the arm she was holding and kept his body between them, his gaze locked with Eli's as he said over his shoulder, "*I* make that call, not you."

She huffed out a breath behind him, but relaxed her grip without further protest.

Instead of the expected resentment or even anger, a glint of humor lit Eli's light brown eyes as he asked, "New bodyguard, Bells?"

"Yeah. Eli, meet Dev."

After a thorough once over, the guy stuck out his hand with a grin. "I approve. Blake didn't know how to do his damn job."

"You're not helping, Eli," Shelby complained.

"No," Dev corrected as he shook his hand. "You were right. Eli's good."

They shared a quick nod of mutual respect before he stepped aside and let the guy give her that hug. While they exchanged small talk, Dev took note of all visible entry points.

A few minutes later, they left Eli and headed for the back. As they passed an indoor agility course, Shelby called out a hello to Amy, a brunette in a wheelchair holding the leash of a chocolate lab, and Will, their apparent instructor wearing a sweatshirt, shorts, and a prosthetic leg. Both waved back, and Dev offered a quick nod as he followed her toward the doors that didn't even come close to muting a din of barks, yips, and yelps.

When they pushed through into the kennel area, Loyal's doppelganger looked up from where he knelt on the floor with a German Shepherd puppy. Nearby, a full grown black and tan Shepherd lay on a dog bed, head up, taking everything in with alert, intelligent eyes.

"Morning, Grayson," Shelby greeted. "Hi, Remy."

The dog on the bed thumped its tail twice but didn't move from her post.

Remy of *Remy's Regiment*, he presumed.

"You're early," Grayson replied brusquely. "In fact, after Loyal called a half-hour ago, I didn't expect you at all." His tone held a note of reprimand with that last bit.

"This trip is fully Dev approved," she defended before turning to extend her arm toward him. "Grayson Cole, meet Devante Torrez, family friend and my new, apparently improved bodyguard."

"Apparently?" Dev protested. Shelby grinned, and he shook his head while turning back to offer a hand to her stoic half-brother. "Nice to meet you. Saw you at the wedding but missed the introductions."

He gave a firm handshake, his lips twisting in a grimace as they released. "I didn't stay long."

Dev had noticed. He didn't know much about him other than mentions his parents had made over the past two years that the guy had not walked into his new-found family with open arms. But he also hadn't asked for more gossip, seeing as it wasn't his business. Now, he found himself more than a little curious about the lingering chilly attitude when *Cole* held first billing on a foundation complex his father had fronted with a hell of a lot of money.

When her brother rose to his feet, Shelby took his place on the floor so the puppy could crawl up onto her lap. "How's little Luna doing today?"

"She's full of piss and vinegar."

"Of course she is, she's a puppy." She hugged the animal to her chest, then laughed when it lunged for the end of her ponytail. When she brushed her hair back over her shoulder, the pup threw its head back with a high-pitched yip, pawed her cheek, and nipped at her chin. "Okay, yeah, you are a handful, aren't you?"

The puppy wiggled wildly, trying to get to her face again. She pulled away with another laugh, and the pure joy in the sound warmed Dev's heart. Her anxiety had relaxed a fair amount since he'd started teaching her self-defense, but the underlying tension never quite bled away. This momentary relief of stress softened her features, letting her natural beauty shine the way it should.

Beside him, Grayson crossed his arms with a soft grunt, and Dev glanced over to find the guy watching him with a narrowed gaze. It was uncanny how much he looked like Loyal. Same Diamond dark hair and brown eyes, brooding brow, and angled jaw covered in a close-cropped beard.

"Doesn't seem wise to have her out right now," her brother stated in a low tone.

"With the schedule switched up, I figured better here than sitting at the house for possible target practice." Movement drew his eye, and Dev followed the progress of a stocky, blond-haired man leading another German Shepherd down the hall toward the doors they'd come through. The guy grinned when he saw Shelby and called out a cheery hello. "And it would appear I have all the back-up I'd need if anyone tried to get to her here."

Grayson gave a tight nod. "You would. Everyone loves Shelby."

Including him, grudging though it appeared. And Dev himself knew all too well how impossible it was not to fall for her.

She shot them a glance as if she knew they were talking about her, and set the puppy down. "I have to get to work, little girl, but I'll come back and play before we leave."

Aware of her brother's keen attention, Dev kept his gaze from lingering when she got up and brushed off the seat of her snug jeans.

"I'm going to try Gus again," he advised. He'd tried to connect with him back at the house, but had to leave a message.

While Shelby and Grayson set up over at a stainless steel exam table, Dev paced to the other side of the room to call the private investigator.

"I just hung up with Mark," Gus answered without preamble. "We got the sonofabitch."

Dev's pulse skipped as he spun to look at Shelby. "He's in custody?"

"As soon as the warrant comes through, the cops are gonna pick him up."

His hope dimmed. A warrant didn't mean shit if they couldn't find the guy. Hell, it didn't mean shit if a judge wouldn't sign it. There would be no relaxing until he was behind bars. "Who is it?"

"Neil Truman—the guy from that letter you had me dig into."

He wasn't surprised. His gut had warned him on that one for a reason.

"The police compared the handwriting from the letter six years ago with the note left at the Diamond estate, and the one on Shelby's windshield," Gus said. "All three matched. What's more, they picked up his car on traffic cam footage a couple miles from the estate and heading in that direction shortly before the break-in this morning, but he lives and works in Boulder."

"Is that enough for the warrant?"

"Damn straight it is. I gotta get going right now, but I'll call you as soon as soon as I know more."

"Thanks."

Shelby happened to look up as he disconnected the call, and their gazes locked. Her quick smile had him praying the faint light at the end of the tunnel got real bright, real soon.

CHAPTER 24

Shelby couldn't help sneaking glimpses at Dev every so often as Grayson brought her the dogs for each well-check. Apparently, she looked often enough that her brother noticed.

"You sleeping with your bodyguard?"

She jerked her gaze back to little Axel on the table as heat seared her face. "No." Although, technically, she was. Just not in the way he meant.

"But you want to."

The warmth in her face spread clear down to her toes. She peered into one of the Shepherd puppy's ears, then the other. "I'm not talking about this with you."

Without lifting his head, Grayson shot Dev a glance where he spoke on the phone while reaching his fingers through the links of a kennel to itch the chin of one of the dogs. "He's into you, too, so what gives? Your dad doesn't approve?"

She gave him the side-eye. "*Our* dad doesn't know, but if he did, he wouldn't care." At least, she was pretty sure he wouldn't care. He wouldn't have allowed them to basically live together if he did, would he have?

No, of course he'd be fine. He and Mom loved Dev and all the Torrezes like they were family.

Shelby handed Axel over for Grayson to switch him out with his sister, Minx. As she started the exam, he braced his palms on the stainless-steel table top. "Is he a good guy?"

There was no holding back her smile as she checked the pup's baby teeth. "Yeah, he definitely is."

Another sideways glance revealed him watching Dev from under his brow.

"What branch did he serve in?"

"Army. Special Forces." Just saying it brought a rush of pride. Special Forces was a big deal. He was brave and tough and—

Grayson grunted.

"Eli likes him," she defended.

That prompted a snort, but there was humor in the sound. "Eli's a vegetarian."

Shelby laughed with her frown. "What's that got to do with anything?"

"Come on now. How much can you *really* trust a guy who doesn't eat meat?"

"That's ridiculous," she admonished.

But secretly, she was enjoying the exchange immensely. It was the first time he'd loosened up enough to joke with her. She'd heard him and Eli trade good-natured insults on numerous occasions, and he relaxed with a few of the other full-time workers, but with her, he'd always maintained a maddening wall of reserve.

His humor remained as she finished with Minx, and

they moved on to Luna. By noon, all the dogs had been checked, and when Grayson asked if they wanted to stay for lunch, she jumped at the chance. Not only was he more unguarded than she'd ever seen him before, he and Dev had hit it off in a way she'd never expected.

Over deep dish pizza, the two talked about their time in the military and swapped a few light-hearted stories. A couple of Dev's questions about the foundation and facilities led to an in-depth tour of the entire campus, and the day practically flew by.

It was nearly four in the afternoon when the three of them sat on the turf floor of the arena with a half-dozen puppies crawling all over them. With the guys still chatting, Shelby played with the puppies as their deep voices ebbed and flowed in a soothing cadence.

Her phone vibrated in her back pocket, and she pulled it out to check the caller. Seeing her dad's number, she slowed the stroke of her free hand over the fuzzy-soft pup sleeping in her lap. "Hey, Dad."

"Hi, hon. How are you holding up?"

"Everything is good here. I'm at the foundation with Dev and Grayson right now." Both of whom fell silent as she added, "How'd the vote go?"

"Good. Your mom and I are on our way to the airport right now. But I called because I wanted to let you know I just got off the phone with the police."

"Any news on the break-in?"

"They caught him, Bells. The guy who broke in and who's been threatening you, they arrested him a half-hour ago. It's over."

She sat frozen as those two words echoed in her head.

Out of nowhere, her chest squeezed so tight she could barely breathe.

"Shelby?"

Dev's voice jolted her attention, and as she met his concerned gaze, she realized her dad was still talking. Somehow she managed to reply, and then told him and Mom to have a safe flight before hanging up.

A smile trembled on her lips as she whispered, "It's over. He said they arrested the guy who's been stalking me."

And then everything went fuzzy as relief swept forward on a wave of overwhelming emotion. Dev was beside her in an instant, passing the puppy from her lap to Grayson before pulling her into his arms. She buried her face against his chest as a sob tore from her throat.

"I'm s-sorry," she stuttered. "This is stupid. I'm happy, and I don't know why I'm crying."

"Stress relief." His voice was matter-of-fact as he rubbed his hand up and down her back. "It's a totally natural reaction. Just breathe through it."

She concentrated on the rise and fall of his chest until a semblance of control returned. With it came a wave of embarrassment. Pulling free from his embrace, she pushed to her feet and turned her back to gather her composure while wiping the tears away.

A moment later, Grayson stood in front of her with two of the puppies. "You good?"

Shelby gave a watery smile. "Yeah."

"Great." He pushed the squirming bodies into her arms. "I'm ready to be done for the day, so let's get these guys put away."

She cuddled the bundles of fur close and forced herself

to meet Dev's gaze as he rose. His expression asked if she was okay, and she nodded. He and her brother scooped up the rest of the pups to return them to their mother, and it was as if her little breakdown never even happened.

Except, Grayson gave her a hug goodbye—a first that nearly brought her to tears again. And as Dev drove home, reality hit on a few fronts. She didn't need his protection anymore. Which meant she didn't need to stay with him anymore. In his house. In his bed.

And speaking of bed...he didn't need to worry about the rest of the world anymore. He could focus on her and only her—if he wanted.

She chose to focus on the reality that didn't have her stomach tangled up in knots.

"I can finally drive my own car again," she mused. "You won't have to chauffer me everywhere anymore."

He shot her a glance, then shrugged. "It hasn't been so bad."

"Says you. I haven't been able to sing car karaoke for over a month."

"No one's stopping you." He gestured toward the radio dial with a smirk. "Pick your poison."

"*I'm* stopping me—and sparing you. You're welcome." The joking didn't help her feel better, so she turned her head as they passed a woman jogging along the sidewalk. All by herself. "You know, we could probably swing by my apartment and get my car right now. I have my keys with me."

Why? Why kick-start the split the second *you don't need his protection anymore?*

Because now that she didn't need him, she was afraid he wouldn't want her. It would be easier to walk away on her own than wait for his rejection.

"I don't want to live there anymore," she continued, "but once I get my stuff from your house, I can go back to Mom and Dad's until I find a new place."

"You have a place."

Dev's firm, almost angry statement lit a spark of hope. When she glanced over from beneath her lashes, he swore under his breath.

"Geezus, what'd you think, I was going to throw you out the second the guy was in jail?"

"Not exactly, but—"

He flipped on his blinker and braked while swerving to the side of the road. She lurched against the seatbelt as he threw the truck in park. A wary glance in his direction revealed his hands tight on the wheel as he glared out the windshield.

"First of all, I know you're itching for your freedom back, but it's going to be at least a few days yet. We have to let everything settle and see if he posts bail."

"Oh. Right." She sank lower in her seat. "I didn't think of that."

"And second…" He unsnapped his seatbelt and twisted toward her while leaning closer.

Her heart stuttered in her chest when he reached to cup her cheek and turn her face to his.

"I don't want you going anywhere now that I can finally do this without feeling guilty."

She had about a half a second to catch her breath before his warm lips covered hers. She tilted her chin up as he slid his hand to the back of her neck. Gentle exploration quickly grew more urgent as he angled his head to deepen the kiss. Shelby opened without hesitation and thrilled at the surge of heat from the deep, bold strokes of his tongue.

Head swimming, she gripped his forearm as a hum of approval vibrated in her throat. When she tried to get closer, the seatbelt held her in place. With a frustrated sound, she fumbled to release it, but Dev caught her hand.

His breath was rough and uneven as he leaned his forehead against hers, eyes closed. After a long moment, he said, "I probably should've waited to do that until later."

Her heart soared at the unconcealed longing in his voice. "I'm glad you didn't."

He smiled, eyes opening as he pressed another quick kiss to her mouth. She leaned forward to maintain contact, and when she tangled her tongue with his, things got hot and heavy again real fast.

With a low groan, he twisted his head to the side and shoved back to his side of the truck. "I definitely should've waited."

Shelby bit the corner of her lip to keep from grinning like a fool, but when he glanced over at her, she ended up laughing anyway. His cute, light-hearted grin nearly had her blurting out how much she loved him.

"If I remember correctly, you packed a dress and heels in your suitcase, didn't you?"

And he said she didn't miss much? "Two dresses," she confirmed.

"What would you say to putting one on so I can take you out for dinner tonight?"

Her stomach gave a nervous little flip as she arched her eyebrows. "Are you asking me out on a date?"

"I am."

Wow. She never would've expected the simple gesture of a date to trigger the rush of emotion that had her blinking against a sting of tears.

"Are you going to say yes?" he prompted.

She nodded, her throat too thick to manage more than a whisper. "Yes."

Was that relief in his grin? She wasn't sure because he turned away to put his seatbelt on, flipped the signal, checked his mirrors, and pulled back onto the road. When they reached his house, he came around to get her door as always, but kept his distance. This time, knowing his reasoning for not touching her and loving why, she didn't take offense.

Inside, she hovered near the door as he reset the security alarm. "So…um…I guess I'll go get ready?"

"Sure." But then he turned with a frown. "Unless it's too early?"

It was almost five o'clock. She shook her head. "Oh, no. I'm going to need at *least* an hour."

"Really?"

"I mean, it is our first date."

When he narrowed his gaze as if trying to gauge her seriousness, she barely kept her poker face in place.

"O-kay then. Let me grab my clothes and the master is all yours for as long as you want."

Fifteen minutes later, Shelby dried off after her shower and belted her robe. She took ten minutes to put on just a light touch of make-up, then another ten to blow dry her hair. Leaving it loose, she turned to eye the two dresses she'd hung in the bathroom to steam out any wrinkles.

Black or burgundy?

Nude.

Stomach whirling, she fiddled with the collar of her robe as the idea spun in her mind. She knew exactly what was going to happen when they got back later, and it was amazingly sweet of Dev to want to take her to dinner first, but did she really want to wait any longer?

No.

Her pulse picked up speed as she crossed the bedroom to her suitcase. Now for the real question—would it still fit?

CHAPTER 25

*D*ev sat on the edge of the couch cushion, flipping through channels on the T.V. while checking the time every two minutes. He still had a good twenty-five minutes to wait, he noted with a grimace. Glancing down the hall, he wondered what the heck she needed a whole hour for? This whole past week, she'd never once taken more than thirty minutes and always looked beautiful on her way out the door.

Turning back to the T.V., he tried a few more channels. Not a single program caught his attention, so he shut it off and tossed the remote on the coffee table before pacing into the kitchen for a drink of water. Then he paced back to the couch.

Fuck, he hadn't been this nervous since...he had no clue when. He'd showered, shaved, and dressed in slacks and a black dress shirt in about ten minutes. Which left him almost the whole hour to sit and think about the upcoming evening.

He was an idiot for torturing himself with dinner, but

after the look on Shelby's face when he asked her on an actual date, he'd endure ten dinners if need be. She deserved to know she was special.

"Dev?"

Shelby's raised voice from the bedroom spun him around. "Yeah?"

"Can you come help me with my zipper?"

Really? Was she trying to kill him? He squeezed his eyes shut, drew in a deep breath, and blew it back out again. "Sure."

He had the entire trip down the hall to mentally prepare for the sight of her, dress unzipped, in his bedroom. The entire hall, and his breath still shortened with every step he took. The door was ajar, and when he pushed it open, he froze on the spot as his mouth went dry.

Holy fuck.

Shelby kneeled on the bed in the late afternoon light, long, dark hair flowing down her back, wearing a nude-colored negligee edged in black lace. The nearly see-through silk stretched taut across her full breasts before skimming down to her thighs.

"I-I didn't want to wait," she said.

He swallowed past the lump in his throat, and then still had to clear it twice before any sound would come out. "Is that the same one?"

She nodded and glanced down as she lifted a hand to fiddle with one of the tiny straps at her shoulder. A grimace flashed across her face, but she lifted her chin and met his gaze. That's when he saw the vulnerability in her eyes and realized the courage it took for her to recreate the scene from nine years ago.

But so much had changed—and thank God it had.

He walked over to his dresser, removing his Beretta and concealed carry holster on the way. After tucking them in the top drawer, he drew in an unsteady breath and pivoted to face her. As he crossed to the bed, he slid his gaze down her body and back up with open appreciation. This time, he didn't want her to have any doubt as to whether or not he wanted her.

His pulse raced as his whole body practically vibrated with anticipation.

"You're as beautiful now as you were then."

She bit the corner of her bottom lip. "It's a little snug."

Only across her breasts. "It's perfect." He reached for her waist, and the heat of her skin seeped through the silky fabric as he urged her forward to the edge of the bed. "You're perfect."

He started to lean down to kiss her, but she pulled back slightly. "Are you okay with skipping dinner?"

"You really think you have to ask?"

"It's just...you're all dressed already—and you look very nice, by the way."

Dev stepped back and stripped down to his briefs in world-record time. As he kicked his pants aside, he said, "There. No longer dressed. Any other questions?"

She shook her head slowly, her gaze dipping down to his chest, then his stomach, and lower. As her attention lingered, he wasn't sure if she was checking out his erection stretching the front of his briefs, or staring at the scars on his left leg. Surprisingly, the second didn't bother him anymore. Not with her.

"You still look just as nice."

The huskiness of her voice sent his blood surging

through his veins as he bumped his knees up against the mattress and reached to pull her to him.

Shelby kept a few inches of space between them, with her palms pressed to his chest. She tilted her head to the side, her gaze sweeping over the floor. "You're just going to leave your clothes and shoes lying all over the place?"

"Right now, I don't give a flying-fuck where my clothes are." He suddenly paused. "Are you making fun of my OCD because you're nervous?"

"A little," she admitted while ducking her head.

He wasn't really OCD, he just liked things put in their place. Usually. When he didn't have much better things to like.

Dev lifted his hand to tilt her chin up with his knuckle, then skimmed his thumb along her bottom lip. When her lashes fluttered down and her lips parted with a shallow breath, he leaned in to fuse his mouth with hers. He teased and nibbled, keeping things soft and gentle until she sighed in surrender, wrapped her arms round his neck, and leaned her whole body into him from breasts to thighs.

Her lips parted, and her tongue sought his, tangling and retreating, luring him in to explore the addicting sweetness of her mouth. He lost himself in the kiss, stroking deep while his hands roamed and caressed, learning her curves and how they fit so perfectly against his angles.

When he palmed her ass and didn't feel the telltale line of panties or a thong through silk, he skimmed up under the hem to find nothing but bare skin. Need flexed his fingers on her firm flesh, and his erection swelled against her belly. The urge to lay her down and bury himself to the hilt made him tremble.

He left her mouth to kiss his way along her jaw, and over to her ear. She raked her nails through his hair, her breath rapid little puffs that revved up his arousal. He worked his way down the delicate line of her throat to the swell of her breasts, then bent to suck one nipple into his mouth through the silky slip.

Her sharp gasp was followed by an inarticulate sound of pleasure. Pulse strumming, he switched to the other side. Her fingers clenched in his hair, tugging at his scalp even as she held him closer.

"God, that feels good," she breathed.

With one hand at her back, he turned just enough to brace his other hand on the mattress to lower her down. Lying beside her, he ran his forefinger along the neckline of her negligee. The material stretched, and he skimmed back and forth, moving farther down with each swipe, until the silk slipped underneath the curve of her breast, leaving the rose-tipped mound exposed in the gathering twilight.

When he moved to do the same to the other side, Shelby asked, "Should I take it off?"

"No way." He watched with mouth-watering anticipation as inch by inch of her second breast was revealed. "I've dreamed about this scrap of silk and lace for nine years, and I'm going to make the most of every second."

Her chest rose and fell with each aroused breath she took, and he drank in the sight of her before dipping his head to run his tongue around the tip of one nipple. He took his time playing and caressing, until she breathed his name again, and he suddenly needed to hear it in the height of her passion.

Dev skimmed his hand down over her belly, dragged the hem of her nightie up, and slid a finger between her folds to find her wet and ready. Her body tensed, but the first skim of his finger over her nub as he sucked hard on her breast had her bucking her hips with a gasp.

Switching sides, he worked her almost to the edge before kissing his way back up to her mouth. Tension gripped her body, and moments later, she bowed beneath his touch as she cried out his name. While she caught her breath, he dug a condom from his nightstand, and stripped off his briefs to roll on the protection. He turned back to find her watching his movements, her expression revealing that seductive mix of innocence and siren from years ago.

She sat up to strip off silk and lace, and then lay back down, her dark hair fanned across the pillow.

He skimmed the vision of her now naked body with a low hum of approval. "Good call."

Then, despite the desperate need thrumming through his body, he trailed a finger from her collar bone to her breast, teased both nipples back into tight little buds, and then skimmed over her ribs and stomach.

"Dev."

His name fell from her lips as a question and a plea. He leaned in to kiss her again, and as her tongue twined with his, he moved over her, nudging her legs apart, easing his tip inside her, until he was right at the moment of thrusting home.

She turned her head just enough to break the kiss. "Dev."

Something in the breathless note of her voice made him still. He lifted his head, his arms trembling slightly with the effort of holding back.

Her expression was a mixture of uncertainty and... guilt? She bit her lip and lowered her gaze as she whispered, "I've never done this before."

It shouldn't have shocked him, yet of anything she could've said, he never expected *that*.

CHAPTER 26

*S*helby held her breath as she waited for Dev's response. She almost hadn't said anything, but if it hurt and she couldn't mask her reaction, she didn't want him to think it was his fault.

Now, as seconds ticked by, she worried he was upset.

"Are you serious?" he finally asked.

She gave a sheepish nod.

"Shelby…all this time?"

The wonder in his voice and implication in his words had her rolling her eyes with a self-conscious little smile. "It's not like I saved myself or anything, it just…never happened, that's all."

Though in this precise moment, she was so very glad it never had.

"Do you want me to stop?"

"No!" she exclaimed when shifted as if he might pull away. She tightened her hold on his shoulders. "No, definitely not. It's just, I've heard the first time can be…not so great, and I didn't want you to think it's you." When his brow furrowed, she quickly added, "But before was…" She paused, and all she could come up with was a slow smile and, "Oh, my *God.*"

His frown cleared with his slight smile. "It's going to be *oh my God* again."

She shivered at the husky promise in his voice and pulled his head down to kiss his lips. "Good, because I want this. *I want you.*"

His mouth covered hers, and once again, his hot, heady kisses consumed her until the whole world was only him as he eased inside her with a slow, rocking motion. There was no pain, only a slight uncomfortable sensation at the tight fit, but that gave way for something more as he moved inside her.

"You okay?" he whispered against her ear.

"Um-hm." She lifted her hips to meet his, and he thrust a little harder. Sensation intensified, and yeah, she could definitely see *oh my God* in her near future.

Buried to the hilt, his sweat-slick body covering hers, he said her name in a gravelly tone that set off a whole host of butterflies in her stomach. She opened her eyes, and when she saw the intensity in his, her pulse skipped hard.

He lifted a hand to brush a stray strand of hair from her cheek, took a moment to tuck it behind her ear, then brought his gaze back to hers. "I love you."

Three little words and she suddenly lost the ability to breathe. Or at least it felt like it with the way her heart was thumping high up in her throat.

"I've loved you since we were kids, I *noticed* you about the time you turned fourteen, which was extremely inconvenient for me at nineteen."

215

"That's why you stopped hanging out with me back then."

He gave a slight smile of confirmation as he bent his head for a feather-soft kiss on her lips. "As I said, *extremely* inconvenient. But *now*...I've been falling head over heels in love with you since you nearly castrated me in the hospital stairwell."

"Let me be the first to say, thank God I didn't."

He chuckled, and the movement of his body rocked him inside her. "You'd be the second, actually."

Grinning, she lifted her knees to settle him deeper, loving the feel of him inside her. A reach of her hand combed her fingers through the hair falling over his forehead as she met his gaze. "I love you, too, Dev. I always have, although what I felt for you at sixteen is a mere shadow of how much I love the man you are now."

Dev leaned down to capture her lips once more, his slow, deep thrusts speeding up, rekindling sensations that had her moving with him as she chased that earlier wave of pleasure. She was close, so close, and when he reached down between them, his touch made her come undone seconds before he followed her over the edge.

By the time she could think straight again, he'd shifted his weight to lay beside her, and she tilted her head toward him on the pillow. "Is it always like that? Because, oh my *God.*"

He grinned. "If it's done right it is."

"Good thing you're OCD."

His chuckle shook the bed. "I'm not really, but I can be on this."

"Yes please," she quipped.

A little while later, she lay with her head pillowed on

his chest as he combed his fingers through her hair. "You hungry?" he asked.

"Getting there, but I don't want to move just yet." She was relaxed and content, and lying with him felt like the most natural thing in the world. It was a moment she wanted to savor for a little longer.

He pressed his lips to the top of her head. "You good with everything?"

She shifted her position to look at him with her palm on his chest, chin on her hand. There was just barely enough light left for her to see his face. "Better than good. You?"

"Same." A smile curved his lips as he brushed his knuckle across her cheek. "Is it too early to talk about where we go from here?"

Her heart thumped against her ribs. "I don't know. You tell me."

His smile faded, and those gorgeous blue-green eyes of his grew somber and serious. "I've never said I love you to anyone else. And I didn't say it to you just because the heat of the moment."

"Me neither."

"Good, because I want more than our first date. I want to be with you for anything and everything. I want to go to bed with you each night, and wake up with you each morning."

"Wake up with me?" she teased, her heart soaring with happiness. "Aren't your military hours going to get in the way of that?"

"Military hours haven't been a thing for me for months. You, however, were just too damn tempting."

"So, it was my fault you were getting up before dawn?"

"One hundred percent. But now, I don't have to anymore." His gaze lowered slightly. "Assuming we're on the same page, that is."

"If you're asking me to move in with you, the answer is yes. If you're asking me to be your girlfriend, the answer is yes. Pretty much whatever you ask me, the answer is yes."

His eyebrows arched high as a smile played on his lips. "*Whatever* I ask?"

"Yes." She held his gaze. "I trust you, Dev, so you don't scare me with that little smirk of yours."

It widened to a grin, and then just as quickly, his expression sobered. "What if I asked you to marry me?"

Geezus. "Are you asking?" she asked breathlessly.

"No, not yet. When the time comes, I gotta do that right."

"Well, I definitely won't argue that," she said. "But just so you know, when the time comes, the answer is yes."

He urged her up for a kiss, then rolled her over onto her back, the full length of his warm, naked body covering hers. "Wanna have sex again?"

"Yes." Then she reconsidered. "After dinner."

CHAPTER 27

onday morning, Dev dropped Shelby off at the animal hospital and then killed a couple hours running errands before driving to the courthouse for Neil Truman's arraignment. Shelby had decided against going, but he wanted to be there when her stalker was put away.

It had been nice to have the weekend off, so to speak. With Truman in jail, they'd been able to relax enough to enjoy the past two days. When they finally dragged their butts out of bed each day, they'd gone for a run/bike ride —she ran while he rode the bike to avoid overdoing it on his leg.

Every day they practiced her self-defense she got better at kicking his ass. Which he was fine with now that she kissed every place she hit—and plenty of places she didn't. Because, like with the self-defense, and he guessed with anything she did, she was a fast study. She was also very thorough, taking her time to explore so she could learn what he liked and what he didn't.

When it came to Shelby, there wasn't much he didn't. She figured out pretty quick how to drive him to crazy, and had employed her new-found knowledge numerous times over the weekend.

Which had more than made up for his one source of anxiety the past three days—telling their families. He'd called his parents before the Diamond family brunch yesterday, and they'd expressed nothing but support and happiness. After seeing them at their dinner the other night, his mom admitted she wasn't even surprised.

Shelby's family, on the other hand, had his stomach tied in knots when they gaped in surprise after she announced they were together as a couple. However, Celia quickly popped up with a happy congratulations and hug for both of them, which spurred everyone else into action. Her dad's welcome had been markedly reserved, but he'd had to excuse himself for a conference call at the end of the meal, so Dev didn't get the chance to speak with him privately before he and Shelby left again.

As he walked up the steps of the courthouse, his gut tightened at the sight of the senator approaching from the opposite direction, his personal protection detail on his heels.

"Morning, sir."

Mark gave a terse nod without correcting him on the formality. A quick word to his detail allowed Dev to fall into step beside him.

Halfway up the stairs, her dad shot him a sideways glance. "Shelby not want to come, or did you make her stay home?"

He bit back a snort at the 'make her' bit. "It was her

choice. She said she'd rather work and do something productive."

The senator nodded.

The obvious chill radiating from the man had him clenching his jaw with resolve. As they reached the top step, he asked, "May I have a minute before we go inside?"

The senator stopped so abruptly Dev had to turn back to face him. Mark dropped any pretense of politeness as he crossed his arms and glared at him.

Knowing exactly the reason for his anger, he got straight to the point. "I didn't act on my feelings for Shelby until after Truman was caught. Her safety was my one and only priority the entire time."

"And what exactly are your feelings for her?"

"I love her," he stated without hesitation. "I've loved her for years."

Mark's gaze narrowed. "You're going to need to explain that a little better, son. You've been gone for years."

"I stayed away because she was too young." A slight ache in his left knee had him shifting his stance as he bit back a grimace. "And once she *was* old enough, it wouldn't have been fair to put her though the worry of wondering if I'd come back every time I left on a mission."

Some of the stiffness left the senator's expression.

"Now that I'm out and have gotten to know the amazing woman she's become, I love her even more."

"So this isn't just a quick little fling after being forced together this past week?"

"No, sir. I promise you, I'd never do that to her."

Mark stared him down for a long moment before conceding with a slight nod of his head. "I respect you,

Dev. Always have. And I trust you—otherwise I wouldn't have put her life in your hands. So as long as you treat her right, we're good."

Relief finally allowed a brief smile. "Thank you, sir."

"Mark." The senator reached out and clapped him on the shoulder, then started inside once more. "Come on, let's get in there."

A half-hour later, they watched as Neil Truman pled guilty to three counts of felony stalking, as well as all the other charges related to his threats against Shelby and the senator. The judge accepted the agreed upon plea deal from the prosecutor, and it was all over in about fifteen minutes.

Surprisingly anti-climatic, but satisfying none-the-less.

Back out on the steps of the courthouse, Dev offered Mark a smile and a handshake. "It's been nice working for you."

Mark chuckled. "I guess we are done, aren't we?"

"Happy it was short-lived."

"Me, too. And if you'd like a letter of recommendation for anything, just say the word."

"Thanks, but working with Shelby actually gave me an idea I'm mulling over. If that doesn't pan out, I'll let you know."

"Sounds good." Mark glanced toward the street as a black SUV pulled up to the curb. "That's my ride back to the office. Give my baby Bells a hug for me."

Dev smiled at the nickname, even as the not so subtle reminder to treat his daughter right rang loud and clear. "I will."

A second later, as he watched the senator descend the

steps, a memory of the message on Shelby's vanity mirror flickered in his mind.

Beautiful silver Bells.

Bells. What was the likelihood Neil Truman knew her family nickname? He supposed a lot of people knew it, like Eli at the veterans foundation. And it was very possible the guy overheard it at an event or something, but...

But no amount of rationalizing could stop the sliver of unease that slid down his spine.

While taking the steps as quickly as possible without his knee giving out, he pulled out his phone and called Gus. The moment the PI answered, he asked, "Do you have a detailed list of what Truman all confessed to?"

"No, but I heard he pled guilty to all charges."

"Yeah, he did, I'm just leaving the courthouse. But there were a few details missing. There was one count of breaking and entering on private property, but they didn't specify if it was for the Diamond estate, or Shelby's apartment. Shouldn't there have been two?"

"Hold on, let me see what I got in my notes." Paper rustled and then he said, "My contact at the department said he copped to the note on her windshield at the hospital, the power steering tampering, and the break-in at the estate."

"And Shelby's apartment?"

"Yeah. He knew where she lived and admitted to being there more than once."

Dev fisted his fingers around his keys in frustration. "But did he actually break-in? Did he write the message on her mirror, or did he just say he'd been there? What about the flowers sent to her at work? The phone calls?

The vandalism at her vet clinic? Did the cops cover all those things in his confession?"

"I do know the vandalism was not him, but I'd have to call my guy on the rest of it."

"Do that," Dev said as he got in his truck. "Call me back as soon as you've talked to him."

"Sure, but...what are you thinking here?"

I'm thinking I let down my guard way too fucking much the second Truman was caught.

A huge ball of lead sunk in his stomach as he said the words out loud. "I think Shelby has a second stalker."

CHAPTER 28

"*I'm so sorry. I'll give you a few minutes to say goodbye.*"

Unfortunately, Shelby had said those words twice in a matter of just three hours this morning. Needing a breath of fresh air, she told her vet tech she was stepping out for a few minutes, and slipped out the back door of the animal hospital into the chilly sunshine. The second worst part of her job was telling someone she hadn't been able to save their beloved four-legged family member. The worst was when she couldn't save them.

The last one had been more heart-wrenching than usual. The family dog had been hit by a car, and the mom had had to bring her two kids along because no one else was home to watch them. Seeing their tear-streaked faces tore at her heart.

She leaned back against the brick wall and closed her eyes while turning her face up to the sun. What she wouldn't give for a hug from Dev right now. The weekend had been amazing beyond what she ever could've dreamed, and as much as she had hated having someone watching her every second of every day, she'd found she'd missed him all morning. Countless times she'd glanced up looking for his handsome face, only to remember he'd gone to the courthouse for the arraignment.

Hopefully, when he picked her up later, everything would be over for good. And even if it wasn't, as long as he held her in his arms and told her he loved her, she'd deal with whatever came next.

"Shelby! Thank God you're here."

The familiar voice jerked her head down, and the sight of Chad hurrying toward her brought a frown. As she straightened from the wall, her stomach gave an uneasy lurch at the sight of his tense expression.

"I need your help," he said in a frantic rush. "Pixie was hit by a car. She's hurt bad."

Hearing the Rottweiler's name, she tensed as she glanced behind him. "Where is she?"

Even as she asked, she spotted Mrs. Walters' Cadillac SUV over by the side of the building, driver's door hanging open, engine still running.

"I have her in the back seat." He started backing toward the vehicle again. "Please help me."

She broke into a jog, pulse picking up speed at the thought of another emergency so soon after the last. "Why didn't you bring her inside?"

"I was afraid to move her."

"Is your grandma okay? Was she with you?"

"No."

They'd reached the SUV by then, and as he opened the back door, she hurried past him to assess Pixie's condition.

But there was no dog in the back seat.

In the split-second she realized her mistake, Chad shoved her face-first against the side of the vehicle. Her cheek hit the glass, and the blast of pain jammed her heart up into her throat, cutting off her breath.

Oh, God, how could she have been so stupid? He was parked too far from the door. In the back of the building —as if he'd been waiting for her. Instinct had told her it wasn't right—that's why she'd asked why he hadn't brought the dog inside. But her emotions had distracted her, and she'd fallen for his excuse to lure her over.

His lips brushed against her ear, his hot breath sending slivers of ice through her veins.

"You should've given me a chance, Bells."

Her nickname in his voice sent an icy chill through her veins. Her cheek throbbed as fear held her paralyzed, her breath rasping in and out of tight lungs, on the verge of hyperventilating. She closed her eyes, desperate to get enough oxygen so she wouldn't pass out.

"Rule number one—use your voice."

She popped her eyes open at the memory of Dev's command. Hope surged, and she focused on controlling her breathing as her mind whirled. She needed air to scream and yell. She needed air to fight.

"Keep your mouth shut," Chad growled in her ear as he yanked her arms behind her back.

The scrape of something over her wrist jolted her pulse, and she struggled to pull away. She couldn't let him tie her hands, and she definitely couldn't let him get her into the vehicle. For a second, she freed one hand, but he grabbed it back before reaching up to slam her head into the SUV again.

Stars sparked in front of her eyes, and tears blurred her vision. "Please don't," she whispered.

He pressed close to her again, the long length of his body against hers turning her stomach.

"Why not me, huh?" Anger roughened his voice. "We got along good. We were friendly during your dad's campaign. I was *always* nice to you, so why the fuck not me?"

Blinking to clear her vision, she judged the distance around the building. It was farther to the front than the back door, but people would be in the front. And if she got free, she could run straight for the corner instead of trying to get around him and the car doors.

"I'm sorry," she whimpered weakly. "I—I—oh, God, I'm gonna be sick."

She dry-heaved, and he backed off just enough to give her the room she needed. Giving a shout that scraped her throat raw, she bent her knees slightly to center her weight over her hips, then pivoted to throw her elbow up into his face with everything she had. He cried out in surprised anger.

Adrenaline twisted her the opposite direction, and she landed a second blow as he grappled for her. Once more in the other direction and she ducked and spun out from in front of him just like she and Dev had practiced dozens of times.

But her shoulder grazed the side of the SUV, throwing off her balance, stumbling her steps. Chad grappled for her, and yelling out again, she swung to land a cupped palm over his ear.

He staggered back, but his bruising grip locked on her arm. When he jerked her toward him, she went for the groin kick. He blocked her knee, and a hard shove bounced her off the SUV, knocking the wind out of her for a terrifying second. As he came at her, she mustered everything she had and used the palm-heel strike up under his chin while screaming so hard her voice broke.

Her blow slammed into his jaw and snapped his head back. When he stumbled backward, she took off running for the front of the building, yelling all the way.

Two steps around the corner, she ran into a wall—a wall of muscle with Dev's voice. "Shelby, it's me. It's Dev. I got ya."

The second her gaze met his, her knees gave out and she sagged against him. He caught her, his eyes frantic as he reached up to gently cradle her throbbing cheek. "Are you okay?"

Her breath caught on a sob of relief as she nodded.

"Stay here." He swung her around, switching their positions to push her into the arms of a man holding a Chihuahua. "Keep her here."

She frowned as he backed away from her. "Dev."

He held out one hand, glancing over his shoulder and as he backed up while drawing his weapon. Meeting her gaze once more, he promised, "I'll be right back, Shelby. Stay here."

And then he was gone around the corner of the building. She held her breath, then flinched when his shout cut through the air.

"Stop right there, Mayer."

A door slammed, and three shots rang out.

CHAPTER 29

Shelby jerked in stunned shock, then cried out and tore free to run around the corner. She slid to a stop when she saw Dev rushing the driver's side door with his gun pointed at the window.

"Get the fuck out and get on your knees," he barked. "*Now.*"

When Chad did as ordered, Shelby noticed the Cadillac sitting at an odd angle. Relief weakened her knees as she realized Dev had shot the SUV's tires.

Police sirens sounded in the distance, getting louder with each passing second. Dev shoved Chad to the ground, kneeled on his back, and bound his hands with a zip-tie—probably the same one he'd tried to use on her. When he started to turn his head in her direction, Dev shoved him face-first into the gravel.

"Don't fucking move, asshole. Your ride's almost here."

The sirens had reached the parking lot by now, and Dev glanced over his shoulder as he tucked his gun away. He grimaced when he saw her standing there watching, but stayed kneeling on her attacker's back with his hands raised as the cops rounded the corner.

One officer went to her, the other advanced on Dev, weapon drawn. Shelby tried to tell them he was okay, but her throat was so raw from yelling, no sound came out.

Dev explained the situation, and a call to the precinct straightened things out in record time. Everything seemed to happen in a fog as the police took their statements, while her alarmed co-workers and curious clients dispersed back inside.

At some point, someone had given her an ice pack for her cheek, and she lowered it when *finally*, she stood by Dev's side as Chad was handcuffed and shoved in the back of the police car.

The moment the squad was out of sight and it was just the two of them, she buried her face against Dev's chest and let her tears flow. He wrapped his arms around her and leaned back against the side of building, almost as if he needed the support, too. She felt his lips against her temple as his hold tightened.

"I'm so sorry I wasn't here for you. I'm sorry I didn't protect you."

The raw guilt in his voice pierced her heart, and she shook her head. When she lifted her face to him, anguish filled his eyes as his hand rose. His fingers trembled, hovering a centimeter from her swollen cheek.

"This is all my fault." Moisture brightened his eyes, and he fisted his hand as his whole body shook against hers with suppressed anger.

"No," she croaked. The pain in her throat made her wince, so she switched to a hoarse whisper. "You are the reason I'm okay, Dev, because you taught me to protect myself."

He frowned, his expression telling her he didn't like her trying to absolve his guilt. But no way in hell was she going to let him take any of the blame.

Holding his gaze, she grabbed his hand and pried open his fist until she could lightly press his palm to her aching cheek. "When he first grabbed me, I froze. I was so scared I could barely breathe, much less scream. But then suddenly you were there in my head, yelling at me about *rule number one,* and I found my voice. And as soon as I found my voice, I started fighting."

The crease in his forehead eased, but not enough. She turned her head and pressed a kiss to his palm. "*You* kept me safe, Dev. You taught me how to protect myself, and you were right there with me in every move I made. That counts double in my book."

He shook his head before pulling her close to bury his face in the crook of her neck while holding tight. After a long moment, he whispered hoarsely, "I don't deserve you."

Shelby smiled slightly and rolled her eyes even though he couldn't see her. "Sure you do."

"No, I don't, but I love the hell out of you, so I'm keeping you anyway."

"I love the hell out of you, too. However..." She pulled back, arching her brow as she tilted her head. "Who said it's your choice? Maybe I'm keeping *you.*"

He gave a wry grin before dropping a feather-soft kiss on her mouth. "In that case, it's definitely your choice. Always."

"I choose you, Dev. It's always been you, and always will be."

She rose up and pressed her mouth more firmly to his. After a long moment, his lips parted and he gently deepened the kiss. The slow, cherishing strokes of his tongue against hers echoed the overwhelming welling of emotion from the depths of her soul.

Her heart was near bursting when he eased back from the kiss and straightened them away from the building. Dev's gaze shifted to her cheek again, and then he bent to retrieve the ice pack she hadn't even realized she'd dropped. A quick swipe against his jeans got rid of any dirt before he pressed it back to her face. "We should go get this checked out."

She made a negative sound while taking hold of the compress. "It's all surface. I'm okay."

"Shelby…"

"I'm good, Dev. I promise." When he still didn't look convinced, she took his hand with her free one and pulled him toward his truck. "All I want is for you to take me home. Just you and me."

He followed as she continued to back up. "We are going to have to call your parents. Not only are they going to want to hear directly from you that you're okay, if your Dad hears about it from the cops first, I'll be back in the doghouse."

Her steps slowed. "When were you were in the doghouse?"

"When your dad thought I was fucking around on the job."

She stopped abruptly, eyes wide. "He *said* that?"

"No, but he didn't have to." He leaned in to drop a kiss

233

on her nose while reaching past to open the passenger door for her. "Don't worry, we cleared the air this morning, and he gave me his blessing."

Shelby felt for the running board with her heel and stepped up so she was looking down at him by a couple of inches. She reached back to toss the ice pack on the seat, then draped her arms over his shoulders. "You didn't *need* his blessing. My dad doesn't get to decide who I date."

"Maybe not, but my future father-in-law's respect matters to me."

Of course it did, and she loved him even more for that. Though the *future father-in-law* had her shaking her head in mock disapproval. "You haven't even asked me yet."

A smart-ass smirk tugged at the corners of his mouth. "And yet you already said yes."

"You still have to ask."

"I will."

"When?" she asked with a grin.

He reached up to pull her arms from around his neck, then clasped her hands together, with his on the outside. His gaze met hers from under his lashes while he pressed his lips to the back of her hands. "When you least expect it."

Which was fine by her. She hadn't expected to run into him in the stairwell at the hospital a month ago. She hadn't expected that he'd become her bodyguard and teach her how to save her own ass.

Most of all, she hadn't expected the man of her dreams would become an amazing reality ten times better than any fantasy she'd ever had.

EPILOGUE

A little over two months later, on a warm evening in early May, Shelby's heart swelled with happiness as a crowd of smiling faces watched her take the makeshift stage Dev had set up for her outside the doors of her new veterinary clinic—and his attached gym. When he hung back at the stairs, she turned from the top with an arch of her brows.

"Come up with me."

"No. This is all you."

Tightening her grip on the oversized pair of scissors in her hands, she tilted her head, but he simply motioned her forward. Knowing it would be quicker if she didn't argue, she formulated an impromptu plan and moved to center stage.

Her pulse sped up as she faced family, friends, and what looked to be an amazing turnout from the local community. If she'd have thought there would be this many people, she'd have gotten a microphone. And a stand to hang on to instead of standing in front of a big red ribbon held on either side of the stage by Eli and Reyes.

"Thank you all so much for coming." Her raised voice came out slightly breathless, and she took a moment to gather her composure before continuing. "Must Love Paws has a simple origin story, but it's no less important. Pets can play a significant role in our lives, and their care has become a booming business that unfortunately not everyone can afford. That was my main goal for opening this clinic.

"Our mission is to provide quality, affordable care for those four-legged fur babies to families who might otherwise have to do without that care, or having a pet altogether. Our client services manager, Megan"—she pointed to the tall, blond college graduate she'd hired two weeks ago—" and the rest of our staff is available today for any questions you may have about what we have to offer and the potential for financial assistance. We're looking forward to working with you and all your babies."

Her dad started a round of applause that swelled through the crowd. Shelby smiled through misty eyes as she waited for it to subside.

"Now, if you'll look to your left..." She gave her guy a proud grin as she swept her arm toward the front entrance to his business. "You'll see we are sharing a building with the brand new Take Control Tactical and Self Defense, run by Special Forces veteran, Devante Torrez. He was kind enough to offer his space for the open house refreshments, and he and his staff of highly trained veterans will also be available to answer any questions you might have about what they offer. I can personally testify, Dev's training is exceptionally effective, and we'll have a special demonstration of his training techniques in, oh, about an hour."

Dev's eyebrows shot up as his gaze locked with hers. "We will?"

"Did I not mention that?" she asked with a heavy dose of innocence.

"No. You most definitely did not."

Laughter sounded from the front, particularly their family members. But she could tell from the glint in his eyes he wasn't really upset. She tossed him a wink, settling into the flow as she turned back to their captive audience.

"Trust me, everyone, you don't want to miss it. And then, last but not least before I cut the ribbon and we get on with this, I want to thank everyone here who helped make this possible either by helping, or offering much appreciated moral support. The cupcakes would go stale if I tried to name everyone, but you know who you are."

She made sure to make eye contact with her parents, siblings and spouses, Elena and Estefan, her sister-in-law's work crew, and then shot a smile to Grayson, who stood off by himself on the side.

"Specifically, I do need to say this would not have been possible without my sister-in-law, Mae, of Lockhart Construction. She and her awesome crew built my beautiful dream clinic in record time. What do you all think? Let's show them some well-deserved love."

Shelby mouthed a *thank you* to her blond sis as Merit raised his fingers to his lips for a piercing whistle and the crowd clapped. When the cheers died down, she shifted her gaze to the redhead standing next to Asher, holding her adorable niece, Ava. "And to my other sister-in-law, Honor, thank you for suggesting and sharing the Must

Love Paws name. I loved it from the second it came out of your mouth."

Honor inclined her head, and they shared a grin.

Returning her attention to the rest of the crowd, Shelby continued, "For anyone who doesn't know, Honor is the owner of the amazing Must Love Frosting Bakery over in our neighboring Lakewood. They're her cupcakes waiting for you next door, so make sure you don't miss out. And without further ado..." She turned and cut the red ribbon, then had to raise her voice over cheers. "Must Love Paws and Take Control Tactical are open for business!"

About an hour later, Dev faced Shelby on the mats of his new gym with a room full of onlookers. She'd pulled her long dark hair up into her trademark ponytail, and joy shimmered in her mischievous brown eyes. This woman kept him on his toes like nothing or anyone ever before, and he loved every minute of it. Every minute with her.

Eli stood on the edge of the mat, waiting for them to begin so he could explain each move as they demonstrated.

Keeping his gaze fixed on Shelby, Dev asked in a low voice, "We'll start here how we first started back in February?"

"Sounds good," she agreed.

There was a little smirk playing about the corners of her mouth that had him narrowing his eyes in suspicion.

"You want to put on the padded suit?" she asked.

"No."

"You want me to pull my punches?"

He gave her a grim smile. "No."

And God bless her, she didn't—until the groin kicks. God bless her indeed.

He chuckled softly as he grabbed her in the bear hug. "Looking out for yourself on that last one, weren't you?" he whispered in her ear.

"That was for both of us, honey-bun."

"Thanks—uuugh." He grunted as she drilled her elbow into his ribs. He'd feel that one in the morning.

He made her work for her freedom this time, and heard a note of frustration in her loud yell as she struggled against his hold. All of a sudden she shifted her weight in a way he wasn't expecting and landed a solid elbow strike to his jaw before twisting free.

Dev lifted a hand to wipe his mouth when she whirled toward him and locked her hands on his wrist. She executed a swift hip swivel/thrust and lifted his arm over her shoulder while twisting her back to him.

Next thing he knew, he was on the ground on his back with the wind knocked out of him. As he struggled to draw air into his lungs, he was distantly aware of the cheers of approval for Shelby, but his focus was narrowed to the sight of her face above him.

"Where the hell did you learn that move?" he wheezed.

"Eli taught me. Didn't expect that, did ya?"

He shook his head and reached to grab the hand she offered to help him up. Instead of getting to his feet, he gave a sharp tug that tumbled them both back down to the mat. She gave a squeak of surprise and braced her free hand next to his shoulder as they landed face to face. The second those beautiful brown eyes of hers met his, he gave her a soft smile.

"Marry me?"

She blinked at the question, and when Dev brought his hand up between them with a square-cut diamond ring pinched between his thumb and forefinger, her eyes widened in shock.

He grinned in triumph. "Didn't expect that, did ya?"

Moisture filled her eyes as she shook her head.

"Oh my, God, he's got a ring."

"He's proposing!"

"She said no."

Shelby dropped her forehead to his chest with a breathless laugh as comments from their audience pierced their private little bubble.

Dev was fairly confident of her answer, but the fact that she hadn't given it yet had his pulse beating a little faster. "Hey." He nudged her shoulder. "You going to leave me hanging here, or what?"

She lifted her head, her eyes aglow with happiness. "You really need to hear it?"

"You wanted me to ask," he countered. "So, unless you prefer candlelight and roses, and me down on my bum knee wincing in pain—"

"Oh, my God, don't be such a drama queen." She giggled, then shifted her body up until her mouth hovered just above his. "Yes, Dev, I'll marry you. Happy?"

"Deliriously."

And he lifted his head for a kiss to seal the deal.

Thank you for reading!

Do you want to help your favorite authors?

Reviews from readers help authors to be able to continue to write the books you love, so I'd be thrilled if you'd let other readers know if you loved Dev and Shelby's story. Please leave a review at your favorite retailer, and copy/pasted reviews to BookBub and Good reads are golden, too.

Thank you so much! ~ Stacey

How can you make sure you never miss a new book?

JOIN my newsletter at www.STACEYJOYNETZEL.com and here's what you get:

*FREE bonus e-books
   *New release announcements
   *what's going on in my writer's life
   *exclusive first-look bonus content
   *cover reveals
   *special sales

Next in the **Must Love Diamonds** series is *Don't Dare a Diamond*, featuring Dev's brother, Reyes, and Shelby's cousin, Raine. Below is your first chapter sneak peek. And, if you haven't read books 1-3 in the series, make sure to check them out, too!

Chapter 1

July
Lakewood, CO

Raine Diamond wasn't used to being ignored. She was the baby of her family, *and* the only girl out of five kids. She'd graduated valedictorian of her class. She was a world-class show jumper, having already won a gold medal in the Youth Olympic Games at eighteen, with aspirations of making the U.S. Olympic team in the near future. Possibly even next year. Her grandfather was a real estate mogul, her parents ran a multi-billion dollar investment firm, and one uncle was a senator, the other head of a jewelry empire.

She was a *Diamond*.

And what was he? A stable boy.

Well...man. A stable *man* who made her pulse race like never before—and that scared the crap out of her.

She fidgeted with seam on the back pocket of her jeans as she stood in her uncle's kitchen with her cousin Shelby, her brother Axel, and Reyes Torrez.

She didn't usually act like an entitled little rich bitch, but for some reason, Reyes triggered the need to prove she was worth looking at. By him. But while her heart went completely haywire at the sight of his thick-lashed green eyes and tousled, sun-kissed, caramel-colored hair, he gave her a cool, heat-inducing once-over, met her gaze long enough for her to offer a nervous smile, and then dismissed her without a second glance.

As he easily joked and laughed with her cousin and brother, she battled a foreign insecurity that left her confused and annoyed. Then he left without so much as a, *"Nice to meet you."*

Who was *he* to act as if she didn't even exist?

If he'd been into Shelby, she'd have understood. Heck, even if he had a girlfriend, he could've simply been pleasantly polite. That's what people did when they met someone new. But the way he'd openly ignored her had been an outright snub. The more she thought about it, the more offended she became.

She stewed all through brunch, only briefly distracted when her cousin Merit dropped a bombshell on the whole family that he and his girlfriend, Mae, were having a baby. Apparently, the girlfriend part had been news, too?

Uncle Mark didn't take it well, and after a dramatic argument, Merit stormed out, Mae followed, then Aunt Janine. After the meal came to an awkward end, her brothers and cousins and their significant others cleared the table and did dishes before settling back around the patio. While they discussed the drama and caught up, she couldn't stop glaring across the lawn toward the stables.

After a few minutes, she got up and wandered inside the house. They were staying one more night, so she'd have plenty of time for visiting, but right now she was restless. Bored with the conversation around the table— and irritated by repeated flashes of Reyes' rude snub.

If only she hadn't sent Diamond Fire home to Texas with their trainer. After they'd won their event yesterday, he'd more than earned a few days rest at home, but now she couldn't go down to the stables with the excuse of checking on her champion baby.

Seeing her mom and Aunt Janine coming down the stairs, Raine seized on a different idea. "Aunt Jan, would it be possible for me to borrow one of your horses for an hour or so?" She rarely went a day without riding, but she couldn't remember the last time she'd been on the back of a horse just for fun.

"Of course." Her aunt gave her a distracted smile, clearly still focused on the earlier brunch drama. "Just ask Estefan or Reyes who could use some exercise."

Her pulse skipped at the mention of the second name. "Thank you."

She hurried upstairs to change and tucked her black V-neck T-shirt into tan breeches before pulling on black,

245

knee-high, leather riding boots. She felt a little bad not asking Shelby to go with her, but her cousin knew her too well and would see right through this move.

When she reached the stables a few minutes later, she had a hard time catching her breath, and it had nothing to do with her speed walk down the curvy driveway. As she approached the open doors, her heart lodged in her throat, and a mass of anxiety writhed in her stomach. She desperately wanted to see him, yet also hoped he was nowhere around, because really, what was she going to say?

Notice me.

Yeah, that wouldn't sound pathetic and self-centered at all.

She stepped inside the barn and scanned for Reyes, only to find the place deserted. Initial relief was quickly replaced by disappointment, until she realized just because she didn't see him didn't mean he wasn't around. Shelby had said he lived in an apartment above the barn.

Squaring her shoulders, she held her chin high as she ventured farther inside. Like at home, the aisles were immaculate, and a deep inhale filled her lungs with the beloved scents of horse, hay, and leather. Heads turned her way, delicate ears swiveling and perking up as pairs of curious brown eyes watched her approach.

She stopped in front of a stall halfway down the aisle and studied the bay thoroughbred inside. The gelding's shiny coat was a rich red, complimented by a silky, jet-black forelock, mane, and tail. He was a big boy like Fire, his withers the same height as her five feet, two inches, putting him at almost sixteen hands tall.

He turned his head with a soft whicker, and she

stepped back when he moved forward to extend his head over the stall door. She let him sniff her hand, then stroked his neck as he lipped at her palm.

"Hello, gorgeous." While rubbing his forehead and laying her cheek against his velvety soft black muzzle, she glanced at the engraved name plate on his stall door.

RazMaTaz.

"Tell me big guy, do they call you Raz, or Taz?" she mused out loud.

"That's Taz."

Her breath caught as she whirled around to see an older gentleman step through a door off to her right. He carried an English saddle over one arm, and a bridle in the other hand.

"Raine?"

"That's me," she confirmed with a smile.

"Hi. I'm Estefan. Janine called and said you were looking for a mount."

Earlier, she'd heard Shelby tell Merit's girlfriend Estefan was Reyes' father. She could also see the resemblance to his son in his olive-toned features and brown eyes from their Spanish heritage. The elder Torrez had a mustache peppered with gray in comparison to his son's neatly trimmed goatee.

"Can I ride him?" she asked hopefully as she stroked the bay's nose. Forget going for a trail ride, she'd love to see what the horse could do on a course.

"Taz is my son's horse," he advised with a hint of apology in his tone. "No one rides him but Reyes."

She blinked in surprise to learn he had his own horse here. None of their employees kept their horses at the

Diamond stables in Texas. Not to mention, the gelding looked to be easily worth twenty grand. Maybe more.

"I'll be saddling Stimpy for you. He could use some exercise."

Stimpy?

Did he not know what she did for a living? She smoothed out her wrinkled nose as she turned, anticipating an old, gentle gelding for beginners.

Estefan slid the stall door open, giving Raine a good look at a regal chestnut with a mass of wavy, reddish-brown mane. Smaller than Taz, the more delicate build and refined features pointed toward Arabian, and she grinned with anticipation. Okay, she could definitely live with Stimpy—which upon a closer look at his nameplate, looked to be short for Rumplestiltskin.

"Your aunt assures me you can handle some fire?"

"Of course." She gave Taz a final, longing stroke along his muzzle before crossing the aisle. "I've been riding my Trakhener, Diamond Fire, since I was seventeen, and I can assure you, he lives up to his name."

He nodded, clearly well-versed with the athletic attributes of her jumper's breed.

"Is it okay for me to take Stimpy out on the trails? Just for an hour or so."

"You remember them?" he asked with an arch of his brows.

"I do. I know it's been a while," she said with a shrug, "but as long as they haven't changed..."

"No, no changes," he assured her. "Warm him up in the arena, get a feel for how he handles, and you should be good."

He wasn't telling her anything she didn't know, but she nodded anyway. "Thanks."

Used to taking care of her own mounts, she stepped forward to saddle the gelding, but Estefan would hear nothing of it. Minutes later, he gave her a leg up and a few tips on the Arabian's personality, then left them with, "Enjoy your ride."

She didn't remember him.

Reyes knew the moment Raine Diamond gave him that warm, interested smile up at the main house, she didn't remember treating him like a smear of manure on the heels of her polished English riding boots during a summer visit ten years ago. His sixteen year old ego had taken a hit, but the memory of two fifteen year old girls drooling over his older brother wasn't what rekindled his resentment after all this time.

It was the fact she hadn't even seen him back then. Dev had been twenty at the time, home on military leave, enjoying his R&R at the pool while hanging out with Loyal and Asher. Reyes had been invisible down in the stables, mucking stalls, sweeping aisles, stacking hay. Fine, he had a job to do. But when he'd finished his shift and joined the rest of 'em, the pretty, brunette Diamond cousin hadn't given him the time of day as she pranced around in her little red bikini.

To her, he'd just been a stable boy. The hired help who'd been shoveling manure while she and Bells went for a joy ride earlier that morning. Of all the years he'd grown up hanging with the Diamond kids, even knowing

249

the gulf of privilege that separated their families, he'd never once felt less than any one of them—until that day.

That feeling came roaring back again today. Didn't matter that he'd caught a flare of interest in the now twenty-five year old's hazel eyes, it was the knowing she didn't recall snubbing him that hit the hardest. To her, he hadn't even been worth remembering.

The irony of that pissing him off was a real kick in the ass. These days, he *wanted* to fade into the background. Since getting out of the Army almost a year ago and coming home, he made sure his usual happy-go-lucky smile and carefree attitude kept everyone from seeing all the shit he kept bottled up inside.

The only one who suspected was Dev, but ninety-nine percent of the time he was training or on a mission, so other than the occasional email or text, he left him alone. The horses were his mental therapy, and with the stables relatively quiet now that the senator and Janine spent a lot of time in Washington, he'd been virtually invisible and glad for it.

One look at Raine up at the main house had set his nerve endings buzzing with energy. His grip tightened on the windowsill of his above-the-stables apartment window as he watched her out in the arena astride Stimpy. Her slim form moved as one with the horse, her long hair streaming out behind her as she cantered him in figure eights with a firm hold on the reins.

The chestnut Arabian could be a headstrong sonofabitch, but right now, he moved willingly under her guidance, his lead switches smooth as butter. Reyes couldn't help but be impressed by her skill and grace in the saddle, though it wasn't surprising given he'd heard

Shelby bragging she was in the running for a spot on the US Equestrian Team.

When she exited the arena for the riding trails surrounding the estate, he headed down to the stables. His gut clenched as his mind screamed to turn around and go back. It reminded him of being on patrol. Trouble was brewing, and he was heading right for it. But he could no more have kept himself from descending the stairs than he could've disobeyed an order from his commanding officer.

The certainty of that left him itchy and restless, and he needed to do something with his hands. In Afghanistan, he used to clean his rifle, and then clean it again. Now, he'd have to make do with saddles. It was almost as good.

In the tack room, he grabbed a cloth and some leather cleaner.

His dad walked by, then back-tracked. Reyes looked up when he stopped in the doorway. "You headed out?"

"Not quite. I'm waiting for Janine's niece to get back from her ride."

"Is Mom done with everything up at the house?" They always rode together when his mom worked on Sundays.

His dad shrugged. "She'll keep herself busy until I can leave."

"You can go if you want. I'll take care of things here."

"Got nothing better to do on your day off?"

Reyes lifted a shoulder as he avoided his dad's direct gaze. "I'm heading out later, so just killing some time for now."

"Hmm." He watched him quietly for a moment.

His pulse thudded hard as he waited for his dad to call him out on the lie.

Instead he gave a shrug. "All right then, suit yourself. Thanks."

It didn't suit him one damn bit, yet there he sat, scrubbing the already shining leather until the light sound of boot heels beat out a rapid rhythm on the cement twenty minutes later. He went on full alert as the steps came to an abrupt halt outside the tack room door.

"Oh. Um...is Estefan here?"

Reyes took his time looking up, partly to make her wait, partly to get his pulse to settle down. But one look at Raine's windblown hair and those bright hazel eyes, and there was no reprieve in sight. "He went home. Why?"

"I was hoping to get some jumps set up."

"Sure." He gestured to the left with the oil cloth in his hand. "Out the main doors, you'll find a large storage room on the left. Jumps are in there. Help yourself."

She blinked at him, her expression astonished. "Help myself?"

"Just make sure you keep them under half a meter. Stimpy doesn't have nearly the same level of training as your jumpers."

One hand propped on her hip, and her brow arched imperiously as her cheeks flushed with color. "You do work here, don't you?"

"I do."

Her gaze narrowed, and he deliberately returned to polishing.

"And you aren't going to at least come help me?"

"I'm busy."

After a long moment, she pivoted on her heel and disappeared toward the storage room. Reyes rested his fist on the saddle with a heavy sigh, waiting for the sound of the wooden rails as she dragged them out to the arena. When all he heard was silence, he conceded maybe he didn't have to be such an asshole because his pansy-ass ego was still bruised from ten years ago. Maybe he should go help—

The clip-clop of horseshoes rang out on the cement.

His brow dipped as he rose and walked to the doorway in time to see Raine leading Stimpy to the cross ties by his assigned stall. She didn't deign to look in his direction as they passed the tack room.

Leaning a shoulder against the doorjamb, he asked, "Change your mind about the jumping?"

"Shelby texted me to meet her at the pool."

Her snooty tone grated across his nerves while his fingers clenched the cloth in his hand at the memory of that little red bikini all those years ago. A mental headshake banished the image as she secured the gelding in the cross ties. Then she gave him a rub on the nose and flipped her hair over her shoulder while turning to walk toward the main house.

Reyes couldn't help but drop his gaze down to the sway of her ass in those tan, skin-tight pants. He swallowed hard against a rising tide of awareness.

"Tell your dad thank you for the ride," she tossed over her shoulder while bending to fish her phone from the front thigh pocket of her breeches.

Reyes tilted his head slightly to watch the stretch of material—until he suddenly straightened from the wall with a jerk of indignation. "Whoa—hold on. Where the hell do you think you're going?"

"To the pool, of course."

"Not before you take care of Stimpy."

"I do believe that's what *you're* paid to do. I'm going to go have a swim."

It was, and it wasn't, but he wasn't about to get into semantics with an uppity little princess like her. *"You're* going to get your ass back here and take care of this horse. Now."

That halted her steps and brought her back around. She lifted her chin, somehow looking down her nose at him from twenty feet away. "You can't talk to me like that. I'll have you fired."

He snorted. "Good luck with that. In the meantime, the rule is, you ride in this stable, you take care of your horse. You may not remember everything about this place, but I know damn well you remember that."

"What does that mean?"

Annoyed with himself for revealing his resentment, he abruptly turned and went back into the tack room.

"I'll have you fired."

The echo of her threat had him clenching his jaw, but he forced himself to take a seat behind the saddle he'd been cleaning and focus on the rhythmic motions of his hand to soothe his pissed-off energy.

While his anger eased, a strange crackle and buzz woke up every cell of his body. The level shot up a notch when, five minutes later, she stomped into the room to deposit Stimpy's saddle and bridle on an empty rack and hook without so much as a glance in his direction. Then she went straight to the bins on the other side of the room, selected the brushes she needed to rub the horse down, and stomped back out again.

See? He shot a narrow-eyed look at the empty doorway. She hadn't forgotten where the brushes were located, and after today, he'd bet a hundred bucks she'd remember him the next time they met.

It could be a year, or another ten, but she'd definitely remember him.

Get *Don't Dare a Diamond* at
www.STACEYJOYNETZEL.com

MUST LOVE DIAMONDS SERIES

ABOUT THE AUTHOR

New York Times bestselling author Stacey Joy Netzel lives in Wisconsin with her family, a horse and some barn cats. She enjoys hiking, canning, and visiting her parents in Northeastern Wisconsin (Up North), at the family cabin on the lake. Travelling anywhere to the mountains to do some hiking is a bonus she wishes she could do much more often than every couple years.

She writes steamy romantic suspense and small town contemporary romances with sexy, rugged heroes, and strong, resilient heroines. Colorado, Wisconsin, and Italy are favorite settings, and you can find them in her Must Love Diamonds, Romancing Wisconsin, Italy Intrigue, Welcome to Redemption Series, and Colorado Trust Series.

www.STACEYJOYNETZEL.com

facebook.com/StaceyJoyNetzelAuthor
twitter.com/StaceyJoyNetzel
bookbub.com/authors/BookBub

ITALY INTRIGUE SERIES

Enjoy a wild ride through Italy full of sizzling, sexy romance and a ton of adventure in this bestselling, award-winning series.

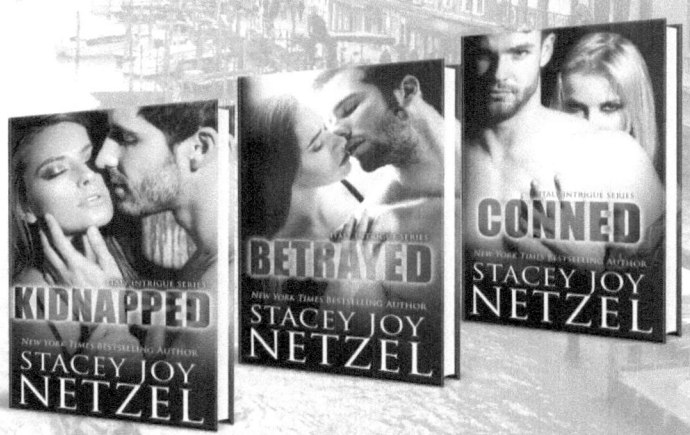

"Gripping romantic suspense in the Mary Stewart mold. Excellent Series!" ~ Helen

Passion flares as bitter enemies race to catch the stallion and win the ranch.

chasin'
MASON

NEW YORK TIMES BESTSELLING AUTHOR
STACEY JOY NETZEL

The writing style of Stacey Joy Netzel captivates me, and her art of telling a great romance story." ~ Danielle, reviewer